MW01110080

John-Richard Thompson's

Best wishes!
John-Richard Thompson

The Christmas Mink

and other December Tales from the North Woods

Illustrated by Jon Robyn

Osiail Publishing

PORTSMOUTH, NEW HAMPSHIRE

Illustrations by: Jon Robyn

Title and headings composed in P22 Victorian
Cover and Book Design by: RPM Ink,
Portsmouth, NH (www.rpmink.net)

Printed in the United States of America

ISBN 978-0-9801992-2-2

Library of Congress Control Number: 2009910091

First Edition

Edited By Josiah J. Eikelboom

Published by:
Osiail Publishing
PORTSMOUTH, NEW HAMPSHIRE
www.osiail.com

Contents

For my parents,
Joan and Edwin Thompson,
for Pat Pomeroy,
and
Uncle Bob

TREE TIME, LONG AGO

The woods await
So come with me,
So come with me to find a tree.
The radio
Predicted snow
Put on your coat, come on, let's go!

Aunt Maudie wants a tree that's small.
Your cousins want a tree that's tall,
But wait and see,
Undoubtedly,
We'll find a tree to please them all.

I've got the axe,
Go call the dog,
We'll circle round the muskrat bog
And find that stand
Of sturdy spruce
Where Uncle Billy saw the moose.

And yes, I know you're only ten
But someday you'll remember when
You came with me
To find a tree
And long to do it once again.

The woods await
So come with me,
So come with me to find a tree!

1

THE CHRISTMAS MINK

I suppose we should get it over with right now - yes, it's true, I *am* a skeptic. And why not? This old world is full of fibbers, exaggerators, and prevaricators. Even here, in this small town in the North Woods, you don't have to wander too far afield to find a so-called friend who will sell you a worthless snowmobile, all the while saying, "but don't she run good though!" and there's me, not a week later, trudging down the trails of Suell's Mountain after the wretched thing sputtered and died up near the power line.

Anyway...let's just agree that we've established this fact: I don't believe most of the things I hear, and those I do, I ponder and examine like an interesting rock, turning it over and over before admitting there might be a grain of truth involved.

Late December is a trying time for us skeptics. We're asked to believe all sorts of fanciful notions, all the way from "no room at the inn", to *ho-ho-ho* coming down the

chimney, to flying deer, all the way to the most fanciful of all, Peace on Earth, Good Will toward Men.

So there I was, one bitter cold night a few years ago, walking down the railroad tracks, out-of-sorts and irritated by the lights blinking in the windows of the houses I passed, with wreaths attached to their front doors like evergreen knockers, and herds of plastic reindeer grazing in snowy dooryards; all the wasteful, frivolous trappings of a holiday soon to come and go. Oh yes, it all looked bright and warm and cheerful, and had I been inside one of the houses I would have joined in the merriment, but I wasn't inside, and all the bright, warm, cheerful sights conspired to make my walk down the frigid tracks all the more dark, cold and cheerless. I tried not to look but I couldn't help it – the snow on the railroad ties had melted, but not on the gravel between them, and this piano-key pattern of snow, railroad-tie, snow, railroad-tie made me dizzy as it passed beneath my boots, so I had to look up.

I don't remember why I was walking down the tracks in the first place. It's likely my car wouldn't start (a car sold to me by the same so-called friend, by the way).

I came to the bend near the pizza place where the wind, no longer broken by trees or houses, tore over the frozen lake like a pack of icy wolves to howl around my ears. I looked out at that island in the middle of the lake, the one where the old camp used to be before it burned ten or so years ago, and where a new fire, a bonfire, now sparked and blazed upon its shore. I saw little ice-fishing houses dotting the lake, some with tiny windows dimly lit by kerosene lanterns, and skaters too, silhouetted against the bonfire, whirling and gliding over a patch of ice cleared of snow. I no sooner saw them when the same wind that made me shiver carried a trace of wood-smoke and frying fish across the ice. *Well, doesn't that smell good!* I thought, and I left the tracks.

Pickerel and trout roasting on snow shovels held over the fire, caught by those kerosene-lit fishermen hunched over their black, slushy holes in the ice: that was the source of the heavenly fragrance. By the time I reached the island, most of the skaters had smelled it too. They joined the fishermen in a circle around the fire, every one of them with a fish-hungry look on their faces as they rubbed their mittened hands together and stamped their boots on the frozen sand or balanced on the tips of their skates like ungainly ballerinas, all the while staring at the coals. I must have stared hardest of all because I can't recall how it started, or who first brought it up.

"Won't be long now," I heard. I looked up from the fire and saw Will O'Dolan sitting on a piece of driftwood, with his wrinkled face lit up inside a curl of pipe smoke like an ancient Micmac warrior. Firelight sparkled on his glasses and he took a long draw on his pipe. The bowl brightened, he let out another cloud of smoke, looked up at the stars and, without taking the pipe from his mouth, said, "Another week or ten days and it will pass over again."

"What will?" I asked, and everyone looked at me.

A young girl wearing a pink coat and a green stocking cap said, "The comet."

"What comet?" I asked, apparently the only one present who couldn't stare at a fire and listen at the same time. Will shook his head in a "nope, I'm not saying it again" way, so the girl took up the slack. "The December comet," she said, and I muttered a scoffing, dismissive phrase or two about how there was no such thing as a December comet because I had never heard of one, seen one, or read of one in any of the scientific periodicals to which I subscribe; and therefore – without seeing, hearing, or reading proof, one had to conclude that such a thing could not possibly exist. Undeterred, the girl said, "It's wicked fast. You have to look real hard, and even then you can't hardly see it."

"No," said an older boy, possibly her brother, "Mr. O'Dolan says you have to believe in it before it comes or you won't be able to see it at all."

"Nobody knows what it is for sure," the girl said with a glance at the old man to make certain she got her facts right. He nodded and she continued, "It looks like a comet because it has a long tail of silver trailing behind it. Right, Mr. O'Dolan? And the tail is some kind of dust or glitter, and when that glitterdust falls, it changes things. It makes the Christmas spirit."

"Oh, I see…" I rolled my eyes. "More Christmas nonsense," I muttered, and turned my gaze back to the fire just as someone passed me a paper plate weighed down with a fish so crispy and hot it crackled and steamed in the air.

"It's true!" the girl cried, and I could tell my skepticism

irritated her. I looked around the fire and was surprised to see a good many others scowling and muttering. I could have let it go, but that's not me. I took off my gloves, broke off a piece of fish, popped it into my mouth and said, "You really believe – oh, that's awfully good pickerel! You *really* believe a silver comet that no one has ever taken a picture of, or seen, or – in my case, even *heard* of until tonight…you honestly believe it leaves a trail of something or other – "

"Glitterdust."

"Yes, yes – and this glitter dust somehow changes everybody?"

"Not everybody," Will said, looking at me for the first time. "And it isn't only people. The changes are made only where the silver dust – or glitterdust, as Mary here calls it – the changes are made only where the silver glitterdust falls."

"Oh, for heaven's sake," I said, and kicked a crust of ice into the fire where it sputtered into steam. "It's not true." I pointed to the sky above our fire, so filled with stars and lights and a great crescent moon that I paused for a fleeting moment, struck by the notion that perhaps I didn't, after all, know all things; but the moment quickly passed, and looking down once more at our fire, so small in comparison but brighter by far than anything the sky had to offer, my thoughts scurried back to the comforting, practical limits of my mind and allowed me to once more laugh at the fanciful visions in theirs. "It *can't* be true."

"Oh, it's all right," said Will to the others. "Leave him be. I didn't believe it either, not at first. And I suppose I'd laugh too if I heard it from someone else instead of seeing it for myself. I'd still be laughing now if I hadn't met the

mink."

"What mink?" I asked, and knew I was in for some real trouble when Mary, the green-hatted girl in the pink coat, sighed impatiently, and said: "He met a mink in the woods who told him about the comet and gave his mother a coat."

Now, friends of my heart, I have already told you how I felt about the comet. Can you imagine how I greeted this new bit of information? With children, sure, I understand their belief in such things, but grown men and women standing around that fire nodded in agreement with Mary as if, sure, of *course* he met a talkative mink — who hasn't — and aren't they a dime a dozen, minks here, minks there, running around the North Woods, chattering night and day? Foolishness, that's what it was. Fool. Ish. Ness. I might have given up and gone home if I hadn't already so happily embarked upon eating my fried pickerel, and yes, I'll admit, if I wasn't a bit curious to hear more...

"This happened to me when I was a boy," Will said, and added with a wink at Mary, "which you can tell by looking at me was a long time ago." To me he said with a touch of defiance: "And you can believe it, or not believe it — it doesn't matter, though I'll say again that it happened to me, and for what it's worth, I can't help but believe it."

I started to speak, but thought I might put myself on stronger footing if I let him tell it all the way through and then came back at him with a point-by-point dissection. Shouldn't be the least bit difficult at all. I bit my lower lip and sat down beside Mary on another piece of driftwood, directly across the fire from Will. She sent a hostile glance my way but didn't flit off to another perch.

This is how he began:

Back in the Depression, in the 1930s…can you kids even imagine a year so long ago? It was a different time then – same town, but a different kind of place. Different time, different place. Most families didn't have much money. The mills had all closed, no one could find any work. My family was poorer than most. We lived out behind the tar-paper factory in a house that isn't even there anymore. Factory's gone too, come to think of it. I had uncles, but they all left to pick potatoes up in Maine for a dollar a day, and ended up staying there. My father had been hurt in a logging accident and couldn't work – he could barely walk, and back then we had no such thing as workmen's comp so made do as best we could. That wasn't easy, considering there were five of us kids.

We gathered spruce boughs in the winter to make wreaths. That brought in a little money for Christmas, and I used to do a little trapping and sell the pelts. Awful business that, trapping. But like I said, those were different times. I got muskrat mostly, and sometimes a beaver, and once in a great while, a mink. Those brought in the most money, mink did.

Trouble was, I only had one trap. I never made enough to buy more traps, and the only way I could think of getting any was to sell more pelts, but without the traps to do it…well…

Another trapper worked the same woods I did. He was a big

burly lumberman from Quebec, came down probably in the early 1920s, with a French accent nearly as thick as his beard; and let me tell you, that beard was thick. Looked like he had a bear cub clinging to his face. Otis LaCranque, that was his name, sometimes called Otis the Crank by us kids, or just Cranky for short. He had a lot more traps than I did and a bigger house than ours. He didn't have nearly as many kids in his family so there weren't too many mouths to feed; but he also had one thing no one else in town had, and no one wanted, and that was Mrs. LaCranque.

Lavinia LaCranque was her name, and oh, let me tell you, she was some piece of work. Given a choice of being married to her or getting run over by the train, I don't know many men who wouldn't have opted for a stroll on the tracks. Women couldn't abide her either. I can't even begin to guess how many conversations at a clothesline started with the words, "you won't believe what *she* did…!"

Thin as a reed, voice rattling like a box of dried peas, a grab-all, penny-pinching, ferret-faced old miser; that was Lavinia LaCranque.

Will paused and shuddered as if remembering some private unpleasantness long past. "My, my…" he whispered before collecting himself again.

They had a boy named Fluey. His real name was Jean-Pierre, but got his nickname because he always seemed to have influenza or the croup. Even when he didn't have a cold of some kind, he still had a runny nose. It was easy to see why: poor Fluey's clothes were so torn you'd see his backside more often than not. We all wore cast offs and hand-me-downs, but at least my mother kept them patched and clean. Fluey's clothes looked like they'd been handed down from a scarecrow, and an unusually shoddy one at that.

My mother called him into our house one morning and made him stand by the wood stove while she mended his britches. That Christmas she knitted him a pair of woolen stockings. She wrapped them in brown paper, wrote *To Jean-Pierre* on the package, and asked me to leave it on their doorstep at night. "Some people are proud," she said at the time. Proud or not, the next day my mother came into the house looking like she might cry and said she had just seen Lavinia LaCranque wearing the stockings meant for Fluey.

The poor kid ended up dying of his nickname that year, though I wouldn't go so far as to blame his mother for that. A lot of people died of the flu that winter – old people mostly, but one or two young ones too. Of course, it was all over town that Fluey died because Mrs. LaCranque wouldn't buy any medicine or pay for a doctor, and I remember one boy telling me he met his demise because she made him sleep out in the woodshed all winter wearing only a horse blanket and no shoes.

The winter after Fluey died, Mrs. LaCranque decided it was time for a new coat. And not just any coat – a *mink* coat! She was a covetous old bird with others, but when it came to her own needs, she was the very soul of generosity. No one in town had a mink coat. Back then, it was hard to imagine anyone *ever* having a mink coat, but that didn't stop Mrs. LaCranque. She told her husband he'd better get her a mink coat or, as she used to rasp, "You'll find out what's good for you!"

I don't believe poor Otis ever did find out what was good for him, though he was threatened with that discovery nearly every day. He didn't know what to do. He certainly didn't have the money to buy a mink coat. He suspected she might have enough squirreled away somewhere, but it was pointless to ask. She would never release the purse strings to that extent, even for her own benefit. He would have to trap the mink himself and, unless he wanted to find out what was good for him, he would also have to find someone to fashion the pelts into a coat. Quite a job, gathering that many minks, but Otis bucked up, squared his shoulders, and went out with a sigh, day after day, to set his traps.

Try as he might, he couldn't catch one. Not one! Christmas was coming and he hadn't so much as a single mink to show for all his work. Day after day, he trudged through the deep snow, and day after day, found all his traps empty. They had been sprung, and the bait taken, but he caught nothing.

Around the middle of December he grew increasingly desperate. Lavinia bore down hard on him. Their neighbors heard her every night, hollering like a banshee. Some came to rely on it to wake them up in the morning, claiming it was more reliable than a rooster's crow, and a darn sight more piercing besides.

One day, a week or so before Christmas, Otis ventured out to check on his traps. First one, empty. Second, empty. Third, fourth, fifth, and on it went, all his traps empty and bare. With only one left to check, he climbed over a small hill near the frozen river and looking down, saw that he had caught something. He clambered down the hill through the deep snow, excited as could be, and even more so when he saw he had trapped a mink. Its hind leg was caught. As Otis raised his club for the kill, it turned and said, "Oh, but really, my good man - would you *really?*"

Otis released the club. His mouth dropped open, and he stepped back with his eyes as wide as an owl's and stared at the little creature in the trap. It was a mink, all right. No question about it. A mink with a red ribbon tied around its neck. That was strange, certainly, and the notion that Otis *thought* he heard it say something was even stranger. But strangest of all was the mink standing up on its hind legs, setting its front paws on its hips and saying: "Well? *Would* you?"

Otis leapt back, startled, and said in stammering French, "Incroyable!" The mink crossed its arms over its chest and looked up at him with an accusatory glare. "Indeed it is," it said, "and if you don't mind, I should like very much to be released from this," it lifted its hind leg and shook the trap, "this incroyably annoying thing."

Otis continued to stare, and though he could hardly bring himself to move a muscle, he nevertheless jumped with a start and nearly ran away when the mink suddenly spread its arms and sang, "*Here we come a-wassailing among the leaves so green–* " It stopped with a sudden quizzical look and scratched its head. "What, pray tell, *is* a wassail?" it whispered to no one in particular, "and how, exactly, does one go about a-doing it?" It snapped two tiny clawed fingers together. "A-ha! Perchance they meant weasel! Makes infinitely more sense I'd say, particularly when the fur-bearing among us raise our voices in song. *Love and joy come to you, and to you a weasel too!*"

Otis feared he had lost his mind. He cried out and turned to run, tripped, and fell headlong into the snow.

"No, no, don't go!" cried the mink, and Otis, crawling backward, whined and blubbered, "But ze minks! Zey do not talk!"

"Zat is true," said the mink, "zo *zis* one do! And now… no, no, *please*, don't go, Otis! Not until you release me, for I should like very much for you to release me. I shan't sing any more, Otis. I promise. And should you remain tormented by the idea of a talking mink, I shan't say another word."

It sat on its haunches and kept its promise – it didn't sing, didn't talk, just sat there in silence, staring with its shimmering black eyes. Otis stared back. A minute passed. No one moved. Another minute passed. They stared. The mink slowly raised a single eyebrow. Otis did the same. Finally, growing impatient, the mink began to hum.

Otis shuddered.

"Oh, all right," the mink whispered, "I shan't do that either."

Otis crawled toward it, slowly. Its rich brown fur glistened with hints of burnished copper in the fading sunlight and he now noticed a sprig of holly attached to its red ribbon collar. He lay down before it in the snow, bringing his eyes level with those of the mink. "What are you?" he asked.

"Mink. Weasel family. Decent swimmer. Partial to

fish."

"No, no, what *are* you?"

"Oh, what *am* I? Well…again - mink, weasel family, decent swimmer, and so forth, but that doesn't really explain things, does it? Not the way you mean anyway." The mink squinted with one eye and tapped its free hind paw on the snow. "Hmmm. What am I…?" It suddenly opened its eyes wide, raised its eyebrows and said, "How's this then? I'm a Christmas Mink."

"Christmas Mink," Otis repeated.

"I may be the only one, for I have never met another. Have you?" Otis shook his head. "I should think not," said the mink. "Therefore, I declare myself - not *a* Christmas Mink, but *the* Christmas Mink. And Otis, surely you realize I can do more than talk, or sing, or hum. Your name, for instance."

"Zat's right! How…?"

"Ahhhh, how do I know your name? Clever how you picked up on that. It's a mystery to be sure." The mink glanced over each shoulder, then lifted a paw and beckoned Otis closer. "And even more mysterious is this: how, I ask you, *how* could I possibly know that your charming wife, Madame LaCranque, desires a coat?"

Otis agreed. "Mysterious…" he muttered.

"I can give her a coat, Otis. I can give her a coat so wonderful, so beautiful, so, so…incroyable that there are no further words to describe the coat I have in mind. I can do it. You know I can. All I ask in return is…" The mink shook the trap again. "Release me, and your wife shall receive all that she has asked for…" the mink bowed with a slight smile, "…and all that she deserves."

Otis rubbed his bearded chin and narrowed his eyes, then shrugged his shoulders and slowly, reluctantly, opened the trap. The mink sprang into the air and bounded across the snow. It hopped onto a snow-covered stump and turned back. "The coat is yours!" it said, and with a cry of, "*Happy Christmas, my good man,*" leaped from the stump and disappeared beneath a spruce bough drooping with snow.

Otis sat beside his empty trap. He looked around for the coat. Long beams of red sunlight passed through the jagged pines, but he saw nothing more. Shadows and cold, an empty trap, and, save for a chickadee flitting from one bare branch to another, stillness. "Talking mink," Otis whispered as if already disgusted with himself for imagining such a thing. He rose to his feet, picked up his trap and his club, and set off for home.

As soon as he left the clearing he noticed something hanging from the snapped-off branch of a birch tree beside the path. His heart leaped with excitement, and he ran toward it, expecting to find a luxurious fur coat, but instead found…well, it was a coat, yes, but one so far from what he hoped for that it might as well have been an old piece of canvas.

Cloth. Dull gray. Several patches of duller gray and black sewn onto it. Torn collar. Frayed sleeves. Worn elbows. "Oh, zat devious little…" Otis muttered. He lifted the coat from the broken branch and rifled through the pockets. Nothing. He pawed the lining. Nothing there either. "Still, it can't be an ordinary coat, not if it came from a mink like zat. Maybe Lavinia will like it," he said, though his heart sank at the thought.

"I'll mink *you!*" she shrieked. "Look at this thing! I ask you for a fur coat and you bring me this, this…*trash!*"

"But zat is what it gave me!" Otis protested.

"Wait 'til you see what *I* give you! Christmas Mink… the only mink you've seen came out of a whisky bottle!" She balled the coat up in her arms and threw it at him. "I don't want it. And unless you'd like to find out what's good for you, you'll bring that atrocious thing back where you found it and bring me what I asked for!"

By this time Otis had had enough of minks and coats and finding out what was good for him, and he trudged back through the dark woods, angrier than he'd ever been before. "Mink!" he sputtered. The cold, clear air did nothing to ease his mind. Indeed, by the time he arrived at the clearing he was so riled with fury that he threw the coat down upon a stone wall and cried, "Zere, you Christmas fibber! You rat in mink's clozing! Take back your coat! I don't want it!"

Night had long since fallen and he could hardly see a thing. Pale moonlight fell upon the clearing, but shadows crowded in, and he was more than a little startled when a small black shape leaped up before him to a level even with his eyes. "Otis?" it asked. It fell back to the ground, and immediately, as though it had springs on its feet, leaped straight up again. "That you?"

It dropped, then sprang up, but before it could say another word, Otis reached out and caught it between his hands. "Oui, yes, it's me," Otis hissed, "and me, I do not zink it was very funny, giving my wife a coat like zat." The mink squirmed out of his hands and fell into the snow. Otis pointed to the coat on the stone wall. "She told me to bring it back and get a better one."

"But that's the only one I have!" said the mink. It seemed surprised and even distressed that someone would refuse such a coat.

"Zen you keep it!" Otis shouted. "I don't want it. I don't want anyzing more to do wiz it, or wiz you! Take it back where you found it!"

"Oh, I couldn't do that," said the mink. "Someone else may want it."

"Zey can have it!" Otis cried, and after muttering a series of foul, pestiferous, French phrases, he turned and stormed from the clearing, leaving the coat and the mink behind."

Will O'Dolan poked the fire with a stick and looked at me as the sparks raced into the air. I could tell by the twinkle in his eye and the half smile that he was daring me to say something, or to laugh, or to argue a point...but no, I had already vowed to wait until he had finished; but oh, how I wanted to say something! The whole time he spoke, a flock of disparaging remarks and contrary opinions fluttered like chickadees through my mind. I calmed them, I fed them seeds of patience, I did everything short of biting my tongue to keep the words from flying free.

I leaned back against the driftwood, silent as a star, and Will took up where he left off.

"This is where I come in," he said, and poked the fire again. Another spiral shot into the sky. Each spark hissed and blazed as it rose toward the stars, and each spark faded and quietly died, disappointed, no doubt, to realize that a star was something more than a reflection of itself. Wind sighed over the lake and the bonfire shivered. "Remember now, I was only ten or so when this happened," Will began.

Christmas was coming, only five or so days away, and things were pretty grim at home. The wreath business was off that year and my trapping hadn't brought in a single cent. I had the same empty-trap trouble as old Otis, though at that time I knew nothing of his run-in with the mink.

My main concern was finding a present for my mother. What a terrible weight on my mind! My father had taken us all aside one night and asked us to do all we could to come up with something special for her.

Let me tell you about my mother. If someone were to ask you to go out and find a person who was all things Lavinia LaCranque was not, you could easily have walked up to our front door, gave it a good knock or two, and when my mother opened it, pointed to her and said, 'There.' She was the kind of person who was happy with whatever you gave her, no matter how simple, no matter how cheap;

but even so, I wanted to give her something special that Christmas, something nice.

I thought and thought as I walked through the woods toward my one lonely trap, but I couldn't come up with a single thing. *Something special*, my father had said, and I searched and I thought and I pondered the issue over and over but came up dry every time. And then I crossed over a small hill and there, draped over a stone wall lay a big grey coat. I couldn't believe my luck! It was patched up in a few places, sure, but it was so thick and heavy that I was certain it would be the warmest coat my mother had ever had. I was about to throw it under my arm and run back to the house when a little mink with a red ribbon around its neck leaped onto the wall beside me.

"Happy Christmas!" it cried, and like Otis before me, I fell back startled into the snow.

"Happy Christmas," I returned in a breathless whisper.

"Like the coat, my boy?"

"Oh, yes, I do," I said. "I'm going to give it to my mother…unless it's yours."

"No, no, not mine. But such a cloth golly-awful grey thing as that? Do you think she'll like it?" I assured him that she would. "Then it's hers!" the mink cried, and he leaped into the air. He did a back flip and landed on his feet again, and I couldn't help but laugh. I rose to my knees before him. "I've never seen…"

The mink rose up on its hind legs and leaned so close I felt his whiskers brush my cheek. Our noses nearly touched. "No doubt," he said. "It is a rare thing to see a Christmas Mink. Uncommonly rare. In fact, you may never see another."

"Where did you come from?"

"These very woods," he said, gesturing toward the trees with his paw. "I was what you might call a run-of-the-mill mink for the longest time; just an ordinary mink with ordinary mink concerns, which, as concerns go, tend to run toward fish...but something happened." The little creature lifted its paws and leaned closer. "Have you heard of the December comet?" I shook my head. "I hadn't either," it said, "but every year the planets and stars and everything else up there gives way for the flight of a small, nearly invisible comet. Most people don't know it exists. Even astronomers with their star-watching machines have seldom found it. The trick of it is, you *can't* find it."

"Then how do you know it's there?"

"Because it *is* there," said the mink. "When I say you can't find it, I mean that no one can come upon it by accident, or think of it as a new discovery. The only possible way to see it is to believe it is already there. That's when it shows itself. And that's when it leaves a great trail of silver dust across the sky."

"Real silver?" I asked, hoping I might find a piece for my mother.

"No, no, no," the mink said, and it sat back and scratched its forehead. "Not real at all."

I too sat back in the snow. "Then what is it?" The mink stepped forward and set its front paws on my knees. "Silver," it said. "Silver dust so fine that it disappears the moment it touches something. For it does touch things, my boy. Falling softly through the night, it falls where it will – it goes into houses and barns, it falls on the pine woods and over the sea. It falls so heavy in some places and spreads a blanket of silver so thick that nothing is left untouched. In other places, only a single speck may fall."

"What is it" I asked again, and the mink pulled back. "The Spirit of the Time," it said.

"Christmas Time?" I asked.

The mink nodded. "That's right. Christmas Time. Christmas Spirit. And what you see before you - me. *I* am what happens when an ordinary mink gets a good dusting."

"Where is it now?" I asked, looking around for a trace of silver.

The mink pulled back and sat on its haunches. "I have no idea. None at all. But let me tell you how it happened. Out for a stroll I was, meandering through the snow, happily warm in my fur, when I took a step and *snap* – right into a trap! Terrible, awful pain," he said with a grimace, and I lowered my eyes. "It wasn't your trap, Will," he said and tapped my knee again with his paw. "It belonged to Otis LaCranque. So there I was, caught in a trap, helpless, when suddenly…hmmm, I don't know what; but *something* happened. I felt a sort of tingly-pingly feeling on my fur, and the pain faded. Silver snowflakes fell from the sky and landed on my fur, on the trap and…that's that! Here I am! Poor Otis. I knew he wouldn't believe any of this so I pretended I was still ensnared in his trap."

"You weren't?" I asked. "Did the silver let you out?"

"Oh, not at all," the mink cried. "The trap let me out. Once touched by the Spirit of the Time, you cannot keep someone confined. Isn't that so, Trap?"

I looked down and saw a bright silver trap beside my boot. It rose up on its chain and began to chatter like a set of false teeth. "How you doin' kid?" it asked. "Merry Christmas."

24

I leaped to my feet. "Merry Christmas," I whispered, stunned, and the mink fell back into the snow, clutching its sides and laughing. "It seems a great clump of silver fell in this clearing. I got the better part of it, but all of us got a speck or two."

The trap agreed. It began to clatter and sing. I looked around the clearing and noticed several spruce trees waving at me. I thought the wind may have been brushing through their boughs, but when I sat on the stone wall, a loose rock swiveled beneath m y hand. It turned up, a crack opened across its width and, in a deep gravelly voice said, "Happy Holidays."

I jumped up again – the woods were alive, I realized, but I wasn't afraid. I don't know why, but I wasn't afraid at all. It seemed more dreamlike than real, as if everything I saw, things without thought or feeling, had suddenly acquired them simply to wish me a merry Christmas. Who could be afraid of something like that?

"You may take the coat," the mink said, reveling in the glorious confusion of the forest clearing. The trees moved, the rocks sang, the trap chattered and shook its chain like a string of sleigh bells, and the mink jumped and flipped in the snow. "And may we send a fond hope that the wearer will find it warm?"

"She will!" I cried, and I jammed the coat under my arm and left the clearing. Shadows deepened in the forest. The sky had dimmed too, with the first stars peeping through the clouds. "Bye Mink!" I called through the trees, and as I passed out of sight I thought I heard a Christmas

25

carol softly drifting through the boughs, but I couldn't be sure. It might have been the wind.

Naturally I couldn't contain my excitement, nor could I help bursting into the house to tell everyone about the Christmas Mink. My younger brothers and sisters believed me and asked me to bring them back to the clearing to meet him. My mother and father smiled at the story, and then: "What's that, Will?" my mother asked, pointing at the balled-up bundle under my arm.

I looked down and nearly fainted. The coat! In my excitement, I hadn't thought to hide it. All the way home I had made plans about how to conceal it and how to wrap it, and I imagined my mother's face when she opened the package on Christmas morning, but it had gone all wrong! I ruined the surprise!

"Oh, it's beautiful!" she cried, and threw her arms around me. "I'm sorry that I saw it, but only because you wanted to surprise me. How on earth were you able to buy it?"

I was so upset I couldn't talk, but Mother didn't seem to mind. She told us how lucky she was that Christmas had come early that year, and she laughed as she put on the ragged old coat and belted it tight. "It's awfully heavy," she said. "I'm sure I'll be warmer than I've ever been, but…my goodness, Will, this is a *very* heavy coat!"

She opened it again and felt the lining. "This is strange," she said, and pulled the cloth back along one of the torn places. We froze then, all of us, as the room brightened. We stared at the lining, sparkling and glittering, touching our faces with light as we gathered around.

"That looks like gold," Father whispered, and his eyes

locked with Mother's before he turned to me, grim and serious. "Where did you get this coat?" he asked.

"I told you, I found it in the woods. A mink gave it to me."

"We can't keep it," Mother said.

"But why?" I cried. "He said it was yours!"

"A coat like this – someone must be looking for it. They may have set it down while looking for a Christmas tree, and planned to pick it up later. No one would have thrown it away."

So there I was, four days before Christmas with no gift for my mother and with the added burden of trying to find the true owner of the golden coat. I went from door to door asking if anyone knew about it. Each person looked at me, then at the shabby coat (more shabby, it seemed, than when I first found it), and said they didn't know anything about it; and more or less indicated they didn't *want* to know anything about it, thank you very much.

Things changed considerably when one of my younger sisters mentioned to a friend that the coat was lined with gold. Within a day we had a line in front of our house that stretched from the door all the way out past the tarpaper factory, with so many now claiming ownership that it was hard to imagine a single garment could have made the rounds so extensively.

Everyone clamored to see the golden lining, and my mother obliged. She put on the coat and walked the length of the line, showing each person the hidden treasure; and

27

it was quite wonderful, to me at least, how that tiny glimpse of gold could jog so many memories. There wasn't a person in line who couldn't tell us where they had bought the coat, how long they owned it, how they lost it, and how, praise God, it was a relief to find it again…but not because of the gold, mind you, no, not at all. "Sentimental value," most claimed. Clearly someone – or rather, many someones – weren't telling the truth, or at best, were mistaken in their claims. We knew almost nothing of the coat, and had no way of knowing if someone had hit upon the truth or not.

"But we *do* know one thing about it," my mother said. "We know where Will found it." She sat in the kitchen with the coat before her, draped over the table, and met with each person in turn. "Where did you leave it?" she asked each claimant, and received answers ranging from the post office to the rear pew in the Sacred Heart Church to the vestibule of the Knights of Columbus Hall, but not a single person mentioned the clearing in the woods.

Finally – and it would have been a miracle if it hadn't

happened – the door swung open with a boom to let in a blast of chilly air followed by the even chillier Lavinia LaCranque. "There it is!" she cried, storming to the front of the line with her husband in tow. "You see Otis? My coat!"

She reached for it but my mother pulled it off the table. "Is it yours, Mrs. LaCranque?"

"Of course it's mine," she snapped. "An early Christmas gift from Otis."

My mother shrank a little, unnerved by the woman's harsh voice. "Please don't be offended," she said, "but I must ask you where you left it. So many have claimed the coat is theirs you see…"

Lavinia LaCranque threw her head back with a haughty scowl then reached behind without looking and grabbed a handful of her husband's sleeve. "Tell her Otis," she said. "Tell Mrs. O'Dolan where you left it."

Otis stepped forward, miserable and cowed, with his hat in his hand. "Well, Mrs. O'Dolan, zere was a mink…"

"Never mind the mink!" Lavinia snapped. "Tell her where you left my coat!"

"In a clearing by ze bend in ze river. I left it on a stone wall while I checked my traps. When I returned, ze coat, it was gone."

My mother turned to me and I thought, oh no, of all people – of *all* people – don't let it be her, not Mrs. LaCranque! "Is that the place, Will?" she asked, and looking down and scuffing the toe of my boot into the floor, I nodded without saying a word.

My mother held up the coat. "Merry Christmas, Mrs. LaCranque. It's a beautiful coat."

Lavinia tore it from her hand without a word of thanks and held it so close it looked like she feared it might squirm out of her arms and crawl behind the woodstove. She put it on and ran her trembling fingers over the sleeves and greedily eyed the lining inside. "Who'd have expected gold from such an ugly coat," she said.

I was still looking at the floor when she reached inside to rip the lining free. I didn't see what happened – I heard it though, a loud gasp from those around me. I reeled back as a terrible stench filled the kitchen. Mrs. LaCranque screamed and pulled her hand from the coat, covered to the wrist with oozing black slime. The lining appeared to melt and then squirm with horrible things, with pale worms and luminous slugs and writhing maggots, all bound within that evil black sludge.

"Get it off me!" screamed Mrs. LaCranque, "get it off, get it off!"

Her husband pulled at the sleeves and my mother held up the lower hem to keep the sludge from oozing onto Lavinia. She pulled free, the coat fell, and, as soon as it touched the floor, the wriggling stopped, the slime melted, and the coat took on the plain, dull, homespun look of before.

My mother lifted it and held it out.

"Get it away!" screamed Lavinia, and hid her face against her startled husband's chest. "I don't want it! Take it away!"

My mother turned to the door but the other claimants had all fled. "I don't understand," she said, and reached inside the coat and felt the lining.

"Don't Ma," I said, but she smiled and said, "It's all right." She put the coat on and pulled the collar up around her neck. "See?" She pulled back the lining and, as before, a warm golden glow filled the kitchen. "I don't understand…" she said again.

Lavinia opened one eye, saw the gold, and in spite of her recent experience, could not contain her greed. She hissed like a cat and reached for it. Her hand touched the lining, a pool of filth opened up at her touch and this time something struck out and bit her.

She pulled her hand back, the pool closed, and Lavinia LaCranque grabbed her husband by the arm and stormed from our house, shrieking and cursing, and threatening to show him, once and for all, what was good for him.

It was a good Christmas for us that year. No one else came by to claim the coat, so we claimed it as our own. My mother wore it nearly every day, though she never took the gold from the lining. She couldn't. Like the silver of the comet, the gold could not be touched. We tried, but whenever a small piece tore free it dissolved into fragments so delicate that they quickly disappeared.

That was fine, Mother told me. It was a warm coat and that was enough.

And maybe it was. Strange things began to happen for us - good things for the most part. A neighbor gave us one of his turkeys for Christmas dinner, and when Mother opened the cigar box she had hidden in the back of the broom closet, she was surprised to discover she had saved far more money than she thought – enough to buy five pairs of new shoes to put beneath the tree. Blessings large and small came day by day: an order for wreaths when none was expected, an offer of payment for me to shovel out a neighbor's walkway, and like Mother's surprise in the broom closet, all of us kids found enough stray money in our pockets to buy our parents something small and good for Christmas.

Something happened to my father too. His injuries, the ones the doctors said would never heal, *did* heal, and it wasn't long before he returned to work in the timber camps.

I can't say with any certainty that the coat or the mink were responsible for any of this. I'm inclined to believe it - these things happened so soon after our meeting - but they seemed also to rise out of our own actions, as though we, somehow, were partly responsible for the good things that happened to us. Who can say? I've seen a Christmas Mink in my life, and can't quite bring myself to deny the reality

of anything after that, no matter how outlandish or foolish it might appear to others.

I returned to the clearing that Christmas Eve. I wanted to see him again and thank him for the coat, and tell him what happened to Lavinia LaCranque (though I suspected he already knew).

It was so quiet in the woods. I heard the snow fall upon the trees with a whispery hush. It was dark too, but the moon, shadowing and brightening behind the snow clouds, lit the clearing in blue. Wind passed through the high spires of pine with a hollow moan, and I wrapped my scarf tight around my neck and pulled my hat down around my ears.

"Mink!" I called. My voice dimmed in the forest, muffled by the falling snow. "Mink! Are you here?"

No answer – snow whisperings and hollow wind, that was all. But then I saw a small dark shape bounding over a stretch of newly fallen snow. "Merry Christmas, Mink!" I called, and I laughed when he reached a deep place and disappeared from view. I ran there and, reaching down with my mittens, I grabbed him around the middle and pulled him up. He shook the snow from his fur. Something jingled from his ribboned collar.

"You have bells!" I cried.

"Why, yes, I do!" he said, and seemed to be as surprised as me. He shook his fur again. "Nothing quite like a sound of bells is there?" I set the mink down on the stone wall and crouched down before him.

"So tell me," he said. "Your mother like the coat?"

"Oh yes! And thank you for letting her keep it."

He cocked his head like a dog hearing a sound it can't understand, so I told him about Mrs. LaCranque. He laughed a bit and then said, "But I had nothing to do with that. It was the coat's doing, not mine."

I didn't understand. "But how…?"

"It's a reflecting coat," he explained. "It gives outer shape to inner thought. Very simple really…well, no, actually, it's not simple at all. In fact, I'd have to say it's one of the more complicated coats one could ever hope to find." We talked a little more, the mink and I, about coats and snow and bells, but soon a wind colder than the others passed through the clearing as if to say, *It's late, Will, go home now, go home…*

"Will you come with me?" I asked.

"Thank you for asking, my boy. Really. I should love it above all things. However…" The mink shook his bells again and bristled his fur until he appeared twice his usual size. "Brrrrr…feel that wind."

I looked up into the trees. "Cold," I said.

He placed his front paws on my mittens. "It's Christmas Eve," he whispered. "Time for us to go."

I didn't understand. "Go?"

"At midnight, my time shall end. All of us - me, Trap, Stone, the trees, everyone touched with silver will have finished all we were meant to do. Enough Spirit will have been spread to carry you through Christmas day."

"But where are you going?"

"I'll fade," he said with a smile and a shrug. "We'll all fade. This holly, this ribbon. Our songs and bells will melt away and all shall become as it was before. Trap will be a trap, and Stone a stone. I will lose my voice and my ribbon and my thoughts. Gone."

"Gone…"

"Yes, but my goodness, don't' think it's over. No, no, not at all! Next December the silver will fall again, and the

world will renew all we feel tonight."

"Will you be here?" I asked.

"Could be! No one knows where it may fall." The mink leaped from the wall and ran into the clearing. "Feel it, my boy!" he cried. "These shreds of silver pass from us to you. Now you must pass them on as best you can."

"How?" I called.

"Feel it!" he called again. "That warm shiver in your heart remains warm only as long as you share it!"

I couldn't see very well in the dark, but it seemed to me he was fading from view; not running beneath a spruce or sinking into snow, but actually losing form and color until he was little more than shadow. "You have no further reason to see me," he called. His voice was a small whisper in the wind, and I heard a tiny, drifting jingle of bells. "But even so, you always will," and with that, he was gone.

I heard only wind then, and snow, and far beyond the dark trees, a rising church bell calling all to Midnight Mass.

Will lit his pipe again and puffed on it. He folded his arms and looked at the fire.

"That's..." I started to say it was nonsense, the most

ridiculous thing I had ever heard, but I stopped and looked around. Mary and the other children sat quiet and thoughtful around the fire. The grown-ups watched the fire and fish with the same thoughtful gaze. How could I say something then? What purpose would it serve to jar the scene with cynical laughter? What reason could I give to break the spell of Will's story, other than to prove I was of stronger mind than they?

I decided to leave them as they were, filled with dreams of talking minks and traps and wondrous coats...and I must admit, I felt a little something too, as though Will's tale was the comet and his words the silver glitterdust, somehow burrowing under my skin and into my blood, until, by the time I left the fire for the mainland shore and stepped off the ice, a feeling had stolen over me.

It's hard to explain, that feeling. What was it the mink told him? That it was a warm shiver in the heart? Yes, that's it. A cold wind still blew from the mountain, but a warm shiver filled my heart as I walked down the railroad tracks for home. I looked at my neighbor's windows without irritation now, and through them saw the red and green of Christmas tree lights. There seemed to be a jingle of bells too, though where they came from, I couldn't tell. Puffs of smoke rose from chimneys and fell again, swirling down from the rooftops to dash across my path like spirits late for a holiday party.

I left the tracks and stepped onto the empty streets of town, silent but for the rhythmic crunch of snow beneath my boots. I passed a stand of snow-covered spruce. A dark shape rose up on one of the lower boughs...I stopped, shook my head and blinked, and walked toward it, slowly, with my thoughts racing - I could almost hear my mind clicking and whirring as it struggled to find a logical explanation.

I reached the tree. Nothing. But there *had* been something there, I was sure of it.

I touched the branch. Heavy clods of snow fell to the ground.

Moments later I passed a fence post and there it was again. I approached and once again it disappeared. I turned a corner and far in the distance, in a pyramid of light and falling snow beneath a streetlight, I saw it clearly, with its ribbon and sprig of holly, standing on its hind legs…but only for an instant before it sprinted out of the light.

I called to it, but heard no answer beyond the rush of snow and the pounding of my own heart in my ears.

I've seen it since then too – many times, year after year, Christmas after Christmas; though I have yet to reach it or hear it speak. It stands always out of reach, and it seems there will never be an answer for me, or at least, none so clear as the ones given to Will in the clearing so long ago.

It may be that the mink knows something I do not, for I do not know how far silver dust falls, or where it falls, or why it falls, though the Christmas Mink seems to have gathered more than his share – so much, in fact, that the mink comes back year after year to spread it around. And I often wonder, as I sit before the fire on a cold December night, surrounded by the sounds of children decorating the tree and windows rattling in the wind, if that warm shiver I feel is all I need ever know from him. That may be the mink's answer, and maybe he knows it's enough.

COAL

Workelf Compensation

~ *Benefits Application Form* ~

NAME: BLIZZARD, JEREMIAH W.

OCCUPATION: ELF

DATE OF BIRTH: JAN. 14, 1843   HT: 3'4"   WT: 66 lbs.

ADDRESS: 712 Ice Mound Way, Unit #45, N.P.

IN THE FOLLOWING SECTION, PLEASE DESCRIBE WORK-RELATED ACCIDENT IN DETAIL.

For the benefit of the ongoing investigation into the reason why the Very Bad Kids (VBKs) did not receive their allotted shipment of coal last Christmas Eve, I respectfully present the following application for Workelf Compensation, submitted in January by one Jeremiah W. Blizzard. It is my belief that the explanation provided by Mr. Blizzard will serve to clear up this matter and bring the investigation to a close in a manner satisfactory to all involved.

Sincerely,
John-Richard Thompson

D ear Respected Members of the Workelf Compensation Board:

I am dictating this to a Snownurse in the Infirmary, as I am unable, due to my extensive injuries, to hold a pen. I am also unable to speak clearly due to the wiring of my jaw, but I shall endeavor to the utmost of my ability to recount - in detail - the events of Christmas Eve last.

The evening in question, December 24th, saw me assigned to coal detail with my former best friend Arthur Sleet. My last Workelf claim took place back in 1912, remembered by some as the year the reindeer flew into the side of the grain elevator, and I have avoided coal detail ever since. Therefore, I was most unhappy to learn that Artie had signed us up. "It will be great!" he told me. "A real change! No more making toys. No more glue all over our fingers. No more walking around yelling *hee-hee* and *ho-ho* for reasons obvious to no one!"

I admit that I too, do not care much for forced elf-laughter. For those members of the Board unacquainted with the finer, more arcane details of Elfinlaw, I respectfully point out that certain regulations passed in the late 1870's state the following: "All elves shall henceforward laugh in manner most jolly at all times, even those when the reason for said laughter shall appear obvious to no one." (Page 758, paragraph 9(c) of addendum 140-968(M), section T98B, *Elfinlaw made Easy*, editor: Alonso Frigid-Smythe). With all due respect to the Board, most elves find this forced laughter a tad oppressive. Even so, I pointed out to Artie that the "real change" he envisioned for us consisted of months at the bottom of a dark filthy coal mine, with few breaks and no days off (the mines have yet to be unionized), searching through the frozen tunnels for stray pieces of coal, gathering them in burlap bags, and – as stipulated in the above-mentioned regulations – we *still* had to laugh. "At all times," I said. "That's what the rule says. *All* times. Even when things are going badly. And if there's something more 'badly' than the lower coal mines, I should like to hear what it is."

It was too late to do anything about it. We were signed up. We had to go. Within days, we found ourselves deep within the twisting, noxious innards of the Badbois Mine, crawling over icy floors, scrounging around for stray chunks of coal in utter darkness (Artie had forgotten to pack the lanterns).

"You wanted a change," I said, my voice echoing in the dank tunnels. My laugh, when I remembered to do it, came out grim and humorless. "No hot chocolate for us, no sir! *Hee-hee.* No hanging out in a warm barn, feeding hay to the reindeer! *Ho-ho-No!* Not for us!"

Artie's voice shivered through the darkness. "Every cloud has a silver lining."

"Oh does it?" I said. "And what, pray tell, is the silver lining in this particularly dark and ghastly cloud?"

"I don't know, but there must be one."

"Maybe it's too dark to see it," I sputtered.

"Maybe so," he said, "but just remember…" He paused, as though reluctant to share his thoughts.

"Remember what?" I asked.

"Every cloud has a silver lining."

I sighed. "And every coal mine has a nitwit." I moved on, crawling and muttering, and feeling for coal. "And who," I said, stopping and turning around in the dark, "*who* thinks *this* is more fun than making toys or hanging out in the barn and feeding the deer?"

"You don't like reindeer," he said, deflecting my question. "Not since they flew into the grain elevator."

"And *who* was driving that night?"

"I didn't know it was a grain elevator. I'd never seen a grain elevator before."

"It makes no difference if you knew what it was or not - you *still* drove into it! Most elves might try to go around it, but you? Oh no, not Artie Sleet. Swerve? Whatever for! Five reindeer and I end up in the infirmary for a month. Well, I tell you this right now: this year I – not you – *I* am driving!"

For those aforementioned members of the Board unacquainted with the finer points of Elfinlaw, those unfortunates assigned to Coal Detail are also assigned their own sleigh and eight tiny reindeer – usually the oldest and lamest in the herd. Our job is to load the sleigh with bags of coal, which generally weigh in at 500 pounds per bag. While Santa and the other elves distribute toys to the Very Good Kids (VGKs), the Coal Elves distribute lumps of coal to the Very Bad Kids (VBKs) and the occasional Horrible Brat (HB). On the surface the job appears fairly easy. We make no decisions concerning which toy to give. We have no worries about where to place them under the tree. The bags are heavy, but elves are strong – especially those without intellectual pretense, like Artie – so we rarely encounter a problem.

This past Christmas Eve, we were assigned a rickety sleigh and eight extremely old reindeer. I can't remember all their names now, though I know for certain that one was Gonner, who is Donner's great-grandfather and simply will not stop talking about it. None of the deer could hear very well. Most of them had no teeth and several had lost their antlers. Two, including Gonner, had cataracts. I put them at the back of the team. "No sense in having blind reindeer in the lead," I said to Artie and - typical - he asked: "Why?"

The two blind reindeer chattered the whole time, with

Gonner being especially talkative: "So I told my great-grandson Donner, I said, 'Dang it, keep your goll-danged head into the wind, and your antlers back,' and so forth."

"What?" asked the other old deer.

"My great-grandson Donner. He works on the lead sleigh."

"Need hay? Donner needs hay? I thought they fed them boys pretty good…"

I buckled them into the harness.

"Hey! What's that?" Gonner cried. "*What's that?*"

"Your harness," I yelled.

"What?"

I ignored him and climbed up onto the sleigh, so loaded down with bags of coal that it groaned and creaked beneath me. Some of the bolts on the rusty old runners had come loose or fallen off, and the whole sleigh leaned to the side.

"Hurry!" Artie said as he scrambled aboard. "Into the air! Hurry! This thing is going to break apart!"

I grabbed the reins and tugged. "On Gonner!" I cried. "On Shlitzen and…and Basher and…all you other guys! *On!*"

The deer stood there, chewing.

"On Gonner!"

"What?" the old reindeer said, turning back to look at us, his cataracts gray and dull in the dim light of the barn. "Who said that?"

I dropped the reins in my lap and turned to Artie. "Get out and tell those deer to move."

He climbed down from the sleigh and trudged to the head of the team. I could see his green pointed hat as he stood in front of the lead deer.

Not at the side. In front.

"Fly!" he yelled. The two lead deer jumped with a startled "hey there!" and leaped forward. Artie's pointy hat disappeared. One of his curly elf shoes poked up through the tangle of harness and bells, and then I heard a horrible *bump-bump-bumpety-bump* under the runners, as we passed out of the barn and then up into the air…but only two feet from the ground. The deer pulled and tugged. We thumped down on the snow, and then up again, struggling to take flight.

"On!" I yelled to the deer. "On! *On!*"

Behind me, I heard "Wait!" and turned to see Artie running after us. He had been pushed down into the snow by the sleigh. His coat was ripped and his hat gone. Large red marks trailed up the side of his face and over his bald head – deer tracks, I assumed. "Look out!" he yelled.

I looked at the path ahead. Three feet off the ground now, we headed straight for the massive rows of silver mailboxes where Santa received his letters from all over the world. "Up!" I yelled. "Up!"

"What?"

Too late. The first deer hit the mailboxes and clattered along the top. The rest followed. Their hooves crashed and clamored on the metal. One of the sleigh runners jammed and pulled the whole row of fifty mailboxes off their wooden frame and into the air, where it trailed behind the sleigh like the tail of a kite. Quite naturally, the sound of this scared the deer, even the *really* deaf ones, and as they flew, they began to look around in an attempt to figure out what it was.

"What was that?" one cried. "Did we hit a plane?"

We flew in a wide circle, three feet off the ground,

dragging our long tail of mailboxes through the snow. Letters and small boxes tumbled in our wake like monstrous snowflakes. Behind this came Artie, fighting through the blizzard of mail.

"The barn!" he yelled, shielding his face from an airborne package. "The barn!"

"What?" I yelled.

"A *plane*, dang it!" yelled Gonner in return. "I asked if we hit a plane! My great-grandson Donner wouldn't hit a goll-danged plane, no sirree, no - that boy can *fly*!"

"The barn!" Artie yelled again.

I turned in time to see my team head straight back into the open door of the barn.

As the Board can see from the documents provided, the main door to the reindeer barn is roughly nine feet high – more than enough room to accommodate a sleigh on the ground. The panel will also recall that we were approximately three feet off the ground, flying erratically. I estimate the height of the reindeer and sleigh to be no greater than five and a half feet altogether. When combining the two figures – three feet of air below and five and a half feet of sleigh, we come to a total of eight and a half feet, leaving exactly six inches of leeway between the top of the sleigh and the heavy wooden lintel that lies across the top of the door opening. I have since calculated my three-foot-four-inch height when sitting and have discovered that the placement of the seat allows exactly eight inches of my head and shoulders to rise above the general height of the sleigh.

Given that there were only six inches leeway between the top of the sleigh and bottom of the heavy beam, but two additional inches of elf, it shall perhaps come as no surprise that my forehead collided with the aforementioned beam with enough force to send me careening backward into the bed of the sleigh. My fur hat cushioned the blow to some extent, though I still have trouble focusing my eyes and have since been unable to get them both to look in the same direction at the same time.

While lying in the sleigh, I heard much shouting and cursing. The main reindeer herd had assembled in the barn to be readied for the Christmas flight, and the sight of our runaway sleigh trailing a clattering line of mailboxes so alarmed them that most took to the air before they were fully harnessed. The barn exploded with flying reindeer, some towing terrified elves behind as they flew over the lofts and between the beams like a flock of panicked swallows, barreling into each other and tangling their traces.

My team dashed out of the barn, still in a state of confusion and panic. None knew where they were or what was going on. "Is this a reindeer game?" one asked above the noise. "I haven't joined in any reindeer games since 1932!"

"What?"

As I lay in the sleigh, blinking and twitching, my reindeer team managed to rise into the air by several additional feet. Artie claims we were now about ten feet off the ground, but still flying erratically. He grabbed a rope from the barn and managed to tie one end into a loop with a slipknot. His intent was to lasso the lead reindeer and rein it in. He therefore waited until we circled around and then threw his rope. Up it went, the deer flew under, and the rope came down, missing all the deer but catching me as I sat up. The noose slipped down over my shoulders and tightened around my chest, pinning my arms to my sides.

I now found myself unable to move my arms and unable to guide the deer, with a 50 foot length of rope and a clanking line of mailboxes trailing behind and, seconds later, Artie too, as he was lifted from the ground, firmly clutching his end of the rope.

"Jeremiah!" he yelled. "Do something!"

"*Do what?*" I yelled in return. "I can't move!" I tried to stand but Artie's weight pulled me off balance. I landed on my back in the bed of the sleigh with my feet straight up in the air.

Before I could move or get my bearings, I heard Artie's voice again – "Turn the deer! Turn the deer!" – and then a terrible crack and crunch as we swerved into one of the enormous, stately Christmas trees in the formal Ice Gardens outside the Claus mansion. The deer made it through the branches, though most were now covered with bits of broken Christmas ornaments and fluttering garlands. The front of the sleigh made it through too. My feet and curly shoes, however, got hung up on a pine bough, which lifted me up and out of the sleigh.

Things might have ended there, but the rope (which remained tightly wound around my chest and arms) became entangled in one of the sleigh runners. This served to create a pulley effect. While I remained behind, caught in the branches of the tree, the sleigh flew forward and the rope passed around the runner so quickly that it began to smoke. Artie, still holding his end of the rope, shot violently past me toward the sleigh. As he whizzed by, I realized his elf training had kicked in and that he was trying to make the best of a dreadful situation. "Hee-*heeeeeeeee!*" he screeched as he tore by, his eyes wide with terror. "Hee-

hee, ho-ho!"

Why he didn't simply drop the rope remains a mystery.

On he flew, catapulting toward the sleigh. I stared in wonder as he slammed against the back, broke through the rotten boards and somehow ended up inside, seated at the top of the coal bags.

The rope tightened.

The slack lifted.

I sat in the tree, still tied to the other end.

"Drop the rope!" I yelled as I watched the slack in the rope lift and lift again and finally straighten as the distance between the sleigh and me widened. "Drop it, Artie!" I shrieked.

"What?"

"Drop – "

Too late. *Whoosh!* Out I flew, dragged into the air and covered with fluttering tinsel. I landed heavily on the ground, but was immediately lifted up again to trail behind the sleigh. I saw Artie through the hole in the back of the sleigh. He was trying to control the deer, but without much effect. They swooped up in an arc and then flew down over a small thicket of undecorated Christmas trees. This action served to loosen the mailboxes, which then flew backward – one by one. As I trailed in their wake, I found myself unable to avoid them all, and, due to my constrained position, unable to fend them off.

Bang. Bang. Bang. The sound of flying mailboxes striking their target filled the air. *Bang. Bang.* And Artie's voice – "You all right?" *Bang. Bang. Bang!*

My reply: "No."

"What's that?" Gonner yelled. "You boys hear

something? What's that goll-danged banging sound?"

"Drop - " *Bang.* "Artie, drop the - " *Bang. Bang.* "Drop the rope!"

"Don't worry!" he yelled. "I'm going to tie this end to a bag."

Surely, I thought – *surely* I had heard wrong. I whistled through the air with mailboxes pummeling me one by one. Surely Artie would realize that the best way to release me from my predicament was to simply drop his end of the rope and allow me to fall gently into the snow. Surely he would not tie his end of the rope to a 500 pound bag of coal. Even Artie wouldn't do that. Surely not.

"There!" he yelled. "Tied nice and tight!"

"Hey!" one of the lead reindeer cried. "What's that thing?"

I peered through the gloom ahead. "It's the toy barn!" I yelled, and visions of my long-ago collision with the grain elevator raced through my mind. "Artie, they're heading for the toy barn!"

"Is that a cloud?" Gonner asked. "Awful big for a cloud."

"It's the barn, Artie! Tell those doddering old deer to swerve!"

Artie climbed onto the seat and cupped his hands to his mouth. "Swerve!" he yelled.

I felt a violent tug. The deer, at the very last moment, finally realized they were flying straight toward a large immovable object.

The two in the lead touched down on the roof but immediately sprang into the air again at a sharp angle. The entire team followed.

My rope swerved up behind them and I followed,

narrowly missing the barn as the reindeer and the sleigh flew straight up like an arrow.

Inexplicably, Artie saw none of this coming. The sharp jolt took him by surprise. He lost his footing and fell out of the sleigh.

I heard a rumble. I opened my eyes and stared at the sleigh shooting straight up into the sky.

I saw the hole made earlier when Artie slammed through the back and the bag of coal, tied to the other end of my rope. I saw the rope tighten, drawing the bag out. And I saw more bags following, each filled with coal, tumbling down through the hole.

Now the sleigh, suddenly released of its weight, sprang forward, catching Gonner and the other elderly deer in the back of the legs. "Hey, hey!" they cried as each pair of deer slammed into the pair in front, and then the entire jumble of fur and antlers met the sleigh, still rushing skyward.

I landed first, gently in the snow, as light as a goosedown feather…and then I heard "Hee H*eeeeeee*!" and saw Artie's face rushing down toward mine, his eyes wide, his mouth open, "Hee hee, ho, h*ooooo*!" and behind him, bag upon bag of coal followed by the broken sleigh and tangled reindeer. I closed my eyes and listened as they fell.

A detailed description of the severity and nature of my injuries is attached. I do hope the Board will favorably review my application for Workelf Compensation, including physical therapy, speech therapy, Post-Traumatic Stress Disorder, and Elfin-Anxiety Syndrome. I thank you for your consideration and wish you a happy and healthy holiday season.

Sincerely yours,

Jeremiah W. Blizzard
Elf

THE CHRISTMAS MICE
OF HARROWBY HALL

At one time, in Harrowby Hall, lived a King
(A blustery, flustery, musty old thing)
Who didn't like this, and who didn't like that,
Who didn't like much but his old yellow cat.

He didn't like carols, and didn't like toys,
He couldn't stand kids (though he had seven boys),
He didn't like winter, or snowmen, or ice,
But one thing he hated above all was mice!

The thought of a mouse, the least indication
Was quite enough to cause heart palpitation.
An actual mouse in the actual attic
Actually gave him a mild heart attatick!

Each winter they came from the moors and the heaths
And tried to build nests in the holiday wreaths.
They hid in the stable and hid in the tow'r.
They hid in the pantry in barrels of flour.

They hid where they could from the king and the cat,
But His Majesty simply would have none of that!
He banished them all, yes he forced them to leave.
He ordered them OUT on a cold Christmas Eve!

His youngest son saw this - his name was Prince Clive.
(Age four and a half – in July would be five)
He saw the mice shivering out in the snow
Running this way and that, with no place to go.

The Christmas Mink

Their tails were all frozen, their noses were blue,
The young Prince could hear their teeth chattering too.
He snuck down the stairs, past the tall Christmas tree
And went to the door in the servant's pantry.

He opened it – called all the cold mice inside,
Said, "Follow me, Mousies! I know where to hide!"
He led them downstairs to a big iron door
And down to a dungeon with bones on the floor!

The mousies were frightened, and Clive understood;
The dungeon was scary, but also was good.
"It's warm here," he told them, "with straw for a nest.
It's dark and it's quiet. That's probably best.

For no one will find you, not even the cat
And I can come visit, I know you'd like that!
I'll bring you some current-cake, bring you some cheese.
I'll even bring cookies, if that's what you please."

And all then was quiet, there wasn't a peep.
The mice were all thawed, and Clive was asleep.
The cat, though, was restless and prowled through the gloom,
Knocked over a lamp in the tapestry room.

It fell on the floor, and the glass chimney broke.
It started to sputter, and started to smoke.
The cat (the old coward) decided to flee
When the lantern rolled under the tall Christmas tree.

A mouse was the first to detect something wrong,
He smelled something burning, he smelled something strong.
He woke all the others, they climbed up the stair,
And squeaked when they saw what was happening there!

The flames were beginning to spread rapidly.
They threatened the presents, they threatened the tree!
There were no alarms, and no bell and no gong,
And no one to warn all inside what went wrong!

And so the mice took it upon their wee selves
To climb up the stairs and to climb up the shelves,
To race up the bell-rope, the curtain, the wall,
And wake all the sleepers in Harrowby Hall!

They started with Clive (as you surely might guess)
Then moved to his mother and brothers and, yes!
They swallowed their pride and forgave and forgot,
And jumped on His Majesty's elegant cot!

They leaped on his belly and pounced on his nose.
They squeaked in his ear and they nibbled his toes.
They pulled on his moustache, his sideburns and beard,
And when he woke up every mouse nearly cheered.

The Christmas Mink

The King, though, was livid and red in the face
"My heavens!" he cried. "They're all over the place!
Begone, little mice, I command you!" he said,
And shooed them and exiled them out of his bed.

And then came the butler who said, "S'cuse me Sire,
It seems, sir, I fear, sir, your castle's on fire."
The king was alarmed and ran into the hall,
The sight that he saw would astonish you all!

He watched from his perch on a high balcony
As the fire leaped up the tall Christmas tree.
The ornaments sparkled, reflected the light,
A red-ribboned gift was already alight.

But what shocked him the most, what held him in thrall,
Was hundreds – no, *thousands* of mice in the hall!
They ran up the tree, bravely facing the blaze
And carried down garlands and tiny glass sleighs.

They rescued the stars, the angels, the fairies,
The trumpets, the tinsel, and strings of cranberries.
They pushed all the presents away, one by one,
And saved all the toys from incineration.

Prince Clive called the King and said, "Papa, look here!"
And pointed above to the huge chandelier.
It was crawling, swarming with little gray things
And moved back and forth as a pendulum swings.

They gnawed at its ropes, and they severed each strand,
While below a door opened – the fire was fanned!
The mice pushed the door! The wind blew inside!
The fire raced up, and the King nearly cried!

But just as it reached to the top of the spruce,
The chandelier toppled, its tether gnawed loose.
It tumbled and landed and fell with a crash,
The tree broke apart, an explosion of ash.

The branches were tossed and they flew through the hall,
Each one burning bright on its tumbling fall,
The mice then attacked them, they ran double-quick.
Each lifted a branch or a twig or a stick.

They carried them burning across the stone floor
Left tendrils of smoke as they ran out the door.
In moments, it seemed, that the last twig was gone,
Now hissing outside in the snow on the lawn.

The King stared and blinked, not believing his eyes.
Said, "Rodents can do *that*? Well, what a surprise!"
Prince Clive knew the reason they risked being burned.
T'was kindness remembered, and kindness returned.

And now every year when the snow starts to fall,
You'll find in the stable, beyond the last stall,
A warm little room full of straw for the guests,
With warm little places for warm little nests.

And in Harrowby Hall, beside the tall tree,
You will find Santa's milk and sugar cookie.
And always beside them, as sure as you please,
A generous platter piled high with Swiss Cheese.

MRS. CAVANAUGH HAD A CAT

I. THE CAROLING PARTY

J. Curtis Smudge detested children. One would never know this from the way he leaped up from his desk to greet those depositors with both large bank accounts and grandchildren. He was all smiles then, a dazzling portrait of patience and good humor. "Oh, what an adorable tyke!" he would cry in a booming, jovial voice. "Look everyone! Look what he's done. Deposit slips aaaall over the floor!"

"Have you grandchildren of your own?" an impressed client might ask on occasion; Mrs. Bulge for example, who has as many grandchildren as she has chins.

"No, no, alas, no," Mr. Smudge might reply. "The Missus and I were not blessed with children of our own, and oh, how I regret it. I regret it deeply. To have missed out on all the, all the – well, as your grandchildren are doing now – all the shrieking and running amok that so warms the heart."

His insincerity was as effective as it was boundless, for J. Curtis Smudge was widely considered a good and industrious businessman; but more to his credit, was renowned as a man who simply adored children. Indeed, his greatest local fame involved children so directly that one can scarcely believe he detested them with a passion generally reserved for rats.

Every December he initiated and led the Christmas Eve ritual known as the Smudge Caroling Party. As President and CEO of First Cranberry Bank and Trust, it was he who first conceived of the idea, and he who led the bundled, chattering herd of unruly youngsters through the snowy streets to bring his wealthiest patrons a small measure of comfort and yuletide cheer.

On this particular Christmas Eve, J. Curtis Smudge and eleven children belonging to a selection of his most prestigious customers, trudged up Harmony Hill Lane, surrounded by breath clouds and all the while clamoring suggestions for the next song. As they crested the hill, they

came upon a dark house set back from the road, unpainted, with windows black and lifeless but for one small, grimy pane near the back whose glow proved so dull and furtive that it looked more like a paler shade of black than anything one might think of as "lit".

The children chattered softly as they passed; this was where the witch lived (every town needs a witch and so everyone knew about the dreadful hag who lurked within the old house, waiting for a chance to waylay children in hopes of catching, cooking and consuming one as required by some dreadful midnight ritual). "Two years ago she chased my brother with a broom," one of the boys whispered darkly. "She caught him throwing snowballs at her birdfeeder and she actually *chased* him with a broom!"

J. Curtis Smudge did not believe in witches, of course. And if such a tale was even partially true, he couldn't have cared less. Whoever lived in the house – witch or not - had neither a checking nor savings account, had never purchased a Certificate of Deposit or IRA, and didn't even belong to the Christmas Club. Why would he bother regaling such a person with music?

At the same time, he actually swelled with the holiday spirit as they passed the sad, dilapidated house, for it marked the place where they first caught sight of the flashing, colored extravaganza that marked the Tipsie residence. By far the wealthiest family in town, the Tipsies put up such a dazzling, flamboyant sideshow every year that any reasonably sane person would find it nearly impossible not to stop and stare and then shake their head in wonder and disgust. Colored lights outlined every line of the house, a plastic Santa and reindeer clung perilously to the roof, and in the front yard stood a crèche so flimsy and with so few walls that one would be hard pressed to determine if the figures inside were meant to represent the Holy Family or members of the Scott Expedition.

J. Curtis Smudge urged his chattering charges past the witch's somber house. Twenty-two little boots and two larger ones scrunched and slipped in the snow as the carolers increased their pace, drawn like frigid moths to the glittering spectacle at the end of the lane. "Now remember, you festive herd of urchins," Mr. Smudge yelled above the din, "we are to do 'Silver Bells' this time."

"Why that one?" asked one impertinent youth.

Rather than explaining his theories regarding the subliminal impact the word "silver" might have upon increased business flow, he simply snapped: "Because I said so," and left it at that. The constant chatter had drained him of holiday merriment. If not for the sight of the Tipsie lights he feared he might resort to swatting one of his charges with the sprig of holly he used as a conductor's baton. But such overt actions could cause trouble with the parents (he knew that well enough), and therefore satisfied his holiday aggression by addressing them with words he felt certain they could not understand. "Come along, my lovely band of vermin," he cried with as much cheer as he could muster. "Don't fall behind. And when we arrive in the dooryard, *do* please remember to caterwaul in your delightfully spasmodic tones."

"But I don't like 'Silver Bells'," pressed the impertinent one. "I like 'Silent Night'."

"So do I," Mr. Smudge said, and added under his breath, "and dearly wish I were having one right now." Once again addressing all the children he said, "I am certain you all have a favorite tune – most young malignancies do – but be that as it may, as I am the leader of this abysmal throng, we shall raise our voices in the song of my choosing," and he intoned rather than sang the opening words: "Silver bells, silver bells, it's Christmas time in the city."

He knocked. The front door opened to send a wave of light over the front steps and J. Curtis Smudge into spasms of cheer. "Merry Christmas!" he cried to the gathering Tipsies, all of whom wore a frown not at all in keeping with the spirit of the season. Mr. Smudge had seen this same reaction year after year. Even so, it took him aback. He did not know what to say. "Yes, yes," he stammered, "Christmas, yes…and yes…round yon virgin, and so forth."

Mrs. Tipsie slapped her hands over her youngest daughter's ears.

"Oh, I beg your pardon," Mr. Smudge said, even more flustered than before. "I meant…oh my. Fa-la-la-la! Yes! So…" He ended with a weak apologetic smile, then turned and lifted his holly baton. "Sing," he hissed to the carolers. "Sing!"

City sidewalks, busy sidewalks, began the children, all of whom (but for two sisters who had once passed through Sherbrooke, Quebec) had never seen a city of any size in their lives.

Dressed in holiday style.

J. Curtis Smudge looked over his shoulder and smiled. "Charming, isn't it?"

In the air there's a feeling of Christmas

The Christmas Mink

The Tipsies never moved a muscle, nor indicated a feeling of *anything* in the air, much less Christmas.

Silver bells. Silver bells!

They stared, unsmiling, with only an occasional shiver to indicate they were alive.

Ting-a-ling. Hear them ring…

"…soon it will be Christmas day," Mrs. Cavanaugh sang in her high, cracked voice. She thought the carolers had passed her house, but couldn't be sure until she heard their distant song. She rose from her chair. "There they are, Maxie" she said, and passed from the living room into the kitchen with her walker clomping down and sliding over the linoleum. She pulled open the door leading out to the side porch, but only a crack, only wide enough to better hear the song.

Mrs. Cavanaugh had a cat, you see. His name was Max, and though he was not the type to bolt and stray, he had a history of charging out the door every Christmas Eve. It never failed: Whenever she opened the door to hear the carolers at the Tipsies, out he went! "No, Maxie," she said, vowing to prevent it from happening this year. "No, pretty boy, no, no, not tonight."

Max rubbed against Mrs. Cavanaugh's spindly ankle. His tail twitched when she pulled the door open a little further, only half an inch.

"Children laughing, people passing, meeting smile after smile," the carolers sang in the distance.

Max looked up at the wall, the way that cats do. He tilted his head. A single Christmas card hung from the windowsill, taped there the day before. He didn't know about such things, of course, but Max thought it was a nice card. It had a bird on the cover. A chickadee. He liked chickadees. He liked the words inside too, printed straight and neat in pale red ink.

Season's Greetings,
Meals-on-Wheels

"...and on every street corner you hear," Mrs. Cavanaugh sang. Max turned his attention to the door. Two inches. Cold reached through with icy fingers. He could see the porch floor dusted with snow and a geranium left out to brown and wither. Was two inches wide enough? No. He wasn't as spry as he used to be, and he doubted he could force it open on his own.

"Eeee-ow," Max whined.

"What, Maxie, pretty kitty? You don't like my singing?" She tapped her fingers against the doorjamb, keeping frail time with the music. "Isn't it lovely? I do wish they would sing 'Silent Night'."

Creeeeeeee – two and a half inches now.

"Maybe some year they'll stop here…"

Creeee – three inches. Enough! Max darted under her walker. If he got his head through she wouldn't close it, he knew she wouldn't.

"Max, no!" cried Mrs. Cavanaugh.

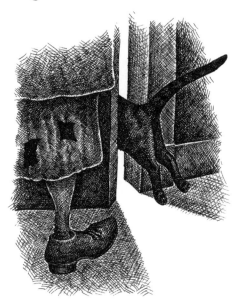

Through! Into the snow!

"No, Maxie – no!" she called, but Max was gone. She pulled the door wide open. "Come back!" Little tracks dotted the shallow snow on the porch, passed down the stairs, dropped into the deeper snow, and disappeared into the darkness of the woods.

II: The Council

Max Cavanaugh ran as fast as he could. His legs ached and his paws hurt. His tail quivered with cold as he padded and bounded through the snow. He would be late. He knew that, but the Council would understand. Cats and dogs were bound by tighter restrictions than most and tardiness was rarely held against them.

Paths of moonlight lay between the pines, and these he followed deeper and farther into the forest where the north wind breathed down upon the trees, and boughs and branches whispered the way, the way to go, *this way* they said in gusty sighs. At last, he broke through a patch of crackling briars into a clearing that glistened with moonlight reflected from innumerable shining things hanging from the trees: silver beer cans; shards of colored glass; lengths of Christmas garland obviously stolen from someone's window; broken Christmas bulbs sharing branches with empty tuna cans; and perched at the top of a small spruce tree, an aluminum tray from a Chinese take-out restaurant, bent and battered into the shape of a star.

The Christmas Council sat beneath the decorated boughs, forming a circle around the edges of the clearing. Some turned to look at Max as he entered and he saw moonlight twinkling in their dark eyes. The rest remained focused on the speaker now holding court in the center of the circle. Max's heart sank, for

the speaker was a wild turkey with his chest feathers puffed and tail feathers spread into a wide, pompous fan. He called himself Tomás (pronounced toe-*mahs*) though he was the only one to do so. His dutiful wife tried to remember to call him by his preferred name, but she, like all the others, had trouble thinking of him as anything other than the far more common "Tom".

Max made his way through flocks of bluejays and chickadees gathered beneath the slender legs of a deer. "S'cuse me. Sorry...pardon me."

A gang of raccoons clicked their tongues and grunted impatiently when he shuffled between them, and he caused a minor ruckus by stepping on the toes of a partridge named Phyllis. "*Do* watch where you're going!" she squawked, startling a herd of jittery rabbits.

"Terribly sorry," Max whispered.

She peered down her beak at him. "As you should be."

Max wriggled his whiskers, and then continued around to the far side of the clearing. "Hi, guys," he whispered when he joined the cats.

The assembled felines nodded. A large bobcat winked at him.

"Hi Bob," Max whispered. "Sorry I'm late."

Bob shook his head and smiled. "What happened?" he whispered. "Old lady keeping you tied down?"

Max laughed this off and said, "No, I had a little trouble getting away, that's all."

"Sure," Bob returned with another wink. "Anyway… you haven't missed much. Tom's been going on for almost an hour."

"Two!" squawked a small mole beside them.

"Yeah, whatever," said Bob and he yawned. The sight of his fangs caused a field mouse to gasp and jab the mole in the ribs. "Shhh, quiet," she said. "Want those teeth coming after you?"

"What teeth?" asked the mole, blinking and searching about.

"On the bobcat."

"What bobcat?" The mole looked up, squinted and leaned forward, nearly touching the object of his search. "Oh, *that* bobcat," he whispered, and was not heard from for the remainder of the evening.

Tom – Tomás – strutted back and forth across the

clearing, expounding, illuminating, and enlightening the forest with eloquence and elucidation. "Ornithologically speaking," the swaggering poultry intoned, "one discovers a certain degree of peccadillo, not to mention an exuberantly sanctimonious hullabaloo."

Max groaned.

"On the other hand, to historicize, to contextualize, and to pluralize by highlighting the contingent, provisional, variable, tentative, and ever-changing is to say, 'Well...you got me!' And one may, or may not, find a panoply – yes, my friends, a veritable panoply – of nothingness as the structural basis of the gewgaw."

"Hear, hear," cried a prickle of porcupines, so caught up in the moment they bristled like pincushions, which persuaded the neighboring raccoons to slide a few inches further away.

"And thus, with the ongoing deconstruction of the eternal monotonies," the turkey began, but when he stopped to take a deep breath in preparation for what promised to be an alarmingly long and complicated thought to come, a massive bull moose (the Council Chairman) stepped out of the shadows. Four sleepy owls, all Committee Secretaries, sat upon his antlers. "This has all been very interesting, Tom," he rumbled.

"Toe-*mahs*."

"Yes, very interesting, *Tom*," the moose said pointedly, "however we have other business to attend to."

The turkey tilted back his head and said, "By which, of course, you mean?"

"Wrap it up."

Tom gazed at the Chairman as if debating whether or not to challenge him, then nodded sharply, cleared his throat and said, "And so, in conclusion – "

The otters in the back rolled around raucously, whistling and applauding. Tom cleared his throat again and glared at them. "*In* conclusion, I should like to acknowledge my lovely wife Sylvia…" At that, a tiny, wattled head atop the scrawniest neck imaginable rose above a pack of muskrats, batted its eyes, and giggled adoringly. "Sylvia," Tom continued, "whose rudiments and steadfast hysteria have been, and remain, a source of inexplicable joy to me."

The Chairman stepped into the clearing. "Thank you, Tom. Most inspiring."

Tom bowed his head sharply and strutted back to his flock.

The Chairman bowed his head in return, which caused the owls to open their eyes in bewildered surprise and turn their heads in all directions. "Now then," the Chairman said, "is there any – you there, in the back, you otters." The giggling, tumbling otters paused in their turmoil. "Stop it," he said with such firmness that they froze and looked at each other with wide startled eyes that quickly brightened with merriment as they tried as hard as possible not to laugh. "Now then," the Chairman continued, ignoring the sound of otters laughing through their noses. "Any old business?"

Voices murmured, antlers tossed, furry heads came together in discussion, and then someone uttered a low

sonorous chirp at the back of the clearing.
"Yes, Your Reverence?" the Chairman said,
and a hush fell upon the gathering.

The cardinal, a dignified old bird,
strolled to the center of the clearing
while three fledglings (whose voices
had not yet changed and
whose feathers showed only
the earliest hints of red)
followed behind, intoning:
*In nomine partridge, et filii et
sparrowus sancti.* The cardinal
held up a red wing, as though blessing the crowd. "*Dominus
chickadeeum,*" sang the fledglings with a bow. "*In spiritus
grousemus.*"

"I should liketh," the cardinal said in deep rounded
tones, "to proposeth a movement, to formally thanketh
the Committium Decoratus, or - in the vernacular – the
Decorating Committee."

"Certainly," said the Chairman, "and I shall second it.
All in favor?" Wings, paws and hooves went up.

"Opposed?" No one but the mole, who most suspected,
had not properly heard the motion.

"The motion has passed," said the Chairman with a
stamp of his hoof. "We hereby offer special thanks to the
crows, led by Miss Ukelele Rook, for their contributions to
this year's spectacular display."

A sleek raucous crow hopped toward the cardinal, threw
a black wing over him (which made him blush, though no
one could tell), and squawked, "Well, that's *awww*ful nice
of you! And me, we, *awwwww*ll of us crows, we are just
– oh, we're just *beside* ourselves!" A collection of crows

proved her right by croaking and hopping and raising a racket. "And *awwwwwwwwll* these trinkets," said Ukelele Rook, "*Awwwwwwwwll* these shiny things we stole...*awwwwww*, er, well, not stole, begging the Cardinal's pardon, we, we –"

The Cardinal bowed his head. "You borroweth without intent to returneth."

"*Awwwwb*viously!" squawked Miss Rook. "And to be fair, I should mention the help given to us by the raccoons and their simply m*awwwww*-velous talent for upending garbage cans." She turned to the staring band of black-masked raccoons and acknowledged them with a gracious nod.

"Like we'd have bothered if there weren't no grub inside," whispered a chubby raccoon named Snout.

The Chairman thanked Miss Rook and the Honorable Cardinal, and asked the assembly if anyone had any new business to discuss. Again – murmurs, nods and antler shakes, but no new business.

"Then I shall make a motion to adjourn and begin the Christmas –"

"Wait!" a small voice cried from the back. "I have a new order of business."

The Chairman tilted his head to the side, which nearly sent one of the owls tumbling backward. "Oh, I say...!" said the owl, who then ruffled his feathers with indignation.

The foxes parted, a deer stepped aside, mice scurried, chickadees hopped, and Max Cavanaugh stepped into the circle. There he stood, surrounded by birds and raccoons and muskrats and beavers, by deer and dogs, mice and moles, and he looked up into the eyes of the enormous

moose with his attending owls. "And you are?" the Chairman rumbled.

"Max," the little cat said. "Max Cavanaugh."

"Oh yes, of course. The one who is always late. My apologies, Mr. Cavanaugh. You are one of our oldest members, are you not?"

Max glanced at all the bright eyes staring at him from the clearing's edge. "I think I must be about the oldest, sir."

"And tell us of this new business you have in mind."

Max brushed his paws over his whiskers. "Well, it's… now remember, I'm not a good speaker, not like Tom is."

Someone applauded. Max suspected one of the otters, as did the Chairman – "Now, now," he warned with a frown before asking Max to continue.

"Yes, sir. Well, you see, it's Mrs. Cavanaugh."

"Hoo?" asked an owl atop the antlers.

"Mrs. Cavanaugh," Max said a little louder. "She lives at the edge of the woods beside the road. I live with her."

"I take it she is one of *them?*" the Chairman asked, his voice a little more grim than before, and when Max nodded, the moose asked: "And what about her?"

Max looked up into the great dark eyes again. He closed his own for a moment, took a deep breath, then turned to the entire council. "She's alone," he began. "Mrs. Cavanaugh is. Except for me. And sometimes another one of *them* comes in to drop some food off, but they don't stay long and don't say much." Max rubbed his paws together. "I know I'm a cat. And I know that you birds don't care much for me when we're not in the Council…but I think you know what I'm talking about. She makes sure you have seeds through the winter. Same for you squirrels. And you dogs…I know she's helped you out too."

The Chairman stepped forward and lowered his head, which was an intimidating sight to be sure, particularly with eight wide glaring owl eyes in addition to his own. "The point, Mr. Cavanaugh?"

"Right," Max said, cowering a bit. "The point." He sat up straight and said, "The point is that I think we should finish the Council out with her."

"Hoo?!" cried the owls, all four at once, and this set up such a hue and cry throughout the clearing that Max crouched and cowered against the Chairman's hoof. He wanted more than anything to dart off into the woods, but he squared his shoulders and stepped out of the Chairman's protective shadow. "Listen," he said to the jeering crowd. "Listen, please!"

They wouldn't. They growled and hissed and chirped and squeaked, all of them, and the forest echoed with the din. Max stepped into the center of the clearing, and there he stayed, silent in the moonlight, watching, waiting, not backing down. Before long they began to settle down, one by one, until the clearing became as silent as the day after Christmas.

Max stared. He took them in, one by one, each shining eye, each furred or feathered face, and then he spoke, "Have you ever wondered why they have never been invited to the Council? Oh sure, I understand the reasons, and I know the rules as well as anyone. But I'm not talking about *all* of them. I'm not talking about the man with that strange smile who sings to the neighbors every Christmas. I'm talking about *one* of them. Only one. Mrs. Cavanaugh. My best friend." He paused, and rubbed his whiskers with his front paw. "She worries about me," he said, and paused again. "I sleep on her lap." He looked down at the snow, unnerved by the staring eyes and dead silence.

A shadow passed in front of his paws.

"Max…" said the Chairman, gently now. "We understand that those who live with them, feel something toward them. But this is the Christmas Council. You know the rules. We gather once a year for a time of truce. At midnight, in only a few short hours, the truce shall end and we return to what we were, to what we truly *are* - with all the hostilities and rivalries of before. The truce is fleeting, and reserved for us alone. Do you understand?"

"Yes," Max said, but then – "No."

"No?" the Chairman asked with the same warning tone he used with the otters.

"No, I don't understand. What's the point of all this if we don't use it for the reason it was given?"

"Which is?" The Chairman leaned down so close that his muzzle nearly touched Max Cavanaugh's nose.

"It's *not* for us alone. It's not only for the contented, or…" he brushed his fur with his front paw, "or the warm. It's for the weak and the lonely too, and the sad. It's something more, something for everyone - not only for us alone. Not for *anyone* alone. It's me, a cat, coming together with Seamus, a sworn enemy since the day I was born."

"And who is Seamus?" asked the moose.

An elderly Irish setter stepped forward, nervous and jittery. "It's meself, sir," he said in a thick brogue. "Seamus Patrick Malone, sir."

"Tell him, Seamus," said Max. "There have been times when she's helped you out."

"There have indeed!" the setter said to the Chairman. "Oh, it was rough. Rough! I'll never forget it, not if I live to be a hundred. There I was, between families, more's the pity, starving – *starving*, I say, with me heart knocking against me ribs, not knowing where me next scrap'a meat was coming from. The shame of the world, that's what it was. And Mrs. Cavanaugh – the very same Mrs. Cavanaugh that Max, here, is telling us about – that dear, sainted lady not only fed me, but gave me a flea bath!"

"And oh, how I hated it," Max said. "Remember how I hissed at you, Seamus?"

"Like a steam engine, you were. And isn't that the God's honest truth?"

Max turned back to the Chairman. "You see? Look around. Foxes and rabbits together. Owls – begging your pardon, your honors – and mice. Me and Seamus. *This* is what it is, who it was meant for. That's the true meaning of a truce. Coming together in peace and friendship with those we would rather avoid or, in some cases, those we'd rather kill and eat."

"No," the Chairman said. "I'm sorry Max. It cannot be. It cannot happen."

Seamus, after a quick jittery bow, rejoined the pack of dogs. Max watched him go and then padded slowly toward the other cats. "May I hear a motion to adjourn?" the Chairman asked.

"Aye," said one of the owls.

"Second?"

A beaver seconded the motion.

"Just a moment!" Everyone turned as an elderly chickadee stepped into the circle.

"You have something to add Mrs. Hopp?"

"Indee-dee-deed I do," said the squat little bird.

She hobbled into the clearing with the aid of small candy cane. "I'm a chickadee-dee-dee. Proud of it. There may be bigger birds, with fancier colors, but as I've always said, 'who gives a hoot?'"

"I do," said one of the owls, believing it was her turn to vote. "Hoot."

"And anyway," the feathered old chickadee continued, "I am as old as Max Cavanaugh, and I have had no warm laps to sleep in, no indee-dee-deed. That was dee-dee-delightful, all that pretty talk to make these folks all weepy, but I know you, Max Cavanaugh. I know what you *are*, Max Cavanaugh. You have had your claws out at me more than once. And I wouldn't trust you so far as I could throw you, which given our sizes, would not be far."

Tomás leaned forward. "Is there a point to all this perpetuity?"

"In-dee-dee-deed there is! And the point is this! As I say, I don't give two hoots about Max Cavanaugh's lap business."

The owls, still confused about the rules concerning the electoral process, offered two additional hoots of their own. *Hoot. Hoot.*

"Please, your honors!" said the Chairman, twitching his ears. "The voting has not yet started. Please continue Mrs. Hopp."

"Long ago – I was little more than a fledgling at the time, a mere slip of a lass – there I was, taking my fill of suet, when suddenly, out of nowhere, a boy threw a snowball at me. Had it hit me, it would most assuredly have resulted in my dee-dee-demise, but what do you think happened? There she was, Mrs. Cavanaugh *herself*, out on the porch, swinging her broom to drive away that dreadful child. Well! Max or no Max, as far as we chickadees are concerned – and I can safely include the nuthatches and titmice in this statement – Mrs. Cavanaugh is a lovely and honorable lady-dee-dee. Not like that Tipsie woman who came at me once with a BB gun."

"Thank you, Mrs. Hopp," the Chairman said, cutting her off. "We've heard all we need. In fact, if we hear any more it will take us past midnight and will make no difference at all. So let's get to it. Mrs. Cavanaugh. The motion is this: should we finish the Council outside her house? Or should we not?" Silence once again fell in the clearing. "Owls?"

The owls blinked. "Hmm? What? Hoo?"

"As Committee Secretaries, you have the first round of voting. Should we end this year's Council at the house of Mrs. Cavanaugh? Aye or nay?"

The owls grumbled and ruffled their feathers and cleared their throats.

"Nay"

"Nay"

"Aye"

"Nay…"

III: THE MOTION

Max padded up the porch steps. Snow, more than before, had blown over the rail into low drifts that looked like the peaks made by pulling a spoon from a vat of whipped cream. He hopped over them and stood before the door with one paw held up.

The door jolted and cracked open.

"Oh, Maxie! Pretty kitty, I've been watching...come, come. Come in out of the cold. Come Maxie."

He didn't move.

"Come kitty."

He sat down. His tail settled on the snow.

"Oh, come Maxie. For heaven's sake, what's gotten into you?"

Mrs. Cavanaugh stepped onto the porch. She hadn't stepped on snow in four years. Her walker sank into the whipped cream drifts. "Max, please...it's so cold."

She reached down, her fingers nearly touching his fur,

but Max stood up and stepped back. She straightened and shook her head in frustration, then took another step.

silent night

Mrs. Cavanaugh froze.

She didn't hear the words, she didn't hear *silent* or *night*…but the sound, the song…

holy night

Something, all around her, in the dark air, in the snow lightly falling…she looked up the road at the Tipsies. Dark. All the garish lights were turned off. The carolers had long since gone home. All was silent.

all is calm, all is bright

"Max…" Her voice wavered. "Come in now."

round yon virgin, mother and child

"Maxie…"

He stepped back again, avoiding her hand. Mrs. Cavanaugh pulled her sweater tightly up around her neck and stared out into the darkness.

holy infant so tender and mild

It was…there *was* something out there. She heard it, a song, a melody, harmony so beautiful…she was nearly ninety-two years old but couldn't remember ever hearing, ever feeling, such beautiful sounds before, such peaceful sounds.

sleep in heavenly peace

She looked down. Max looked up.

And she knew. Somehow she knew…

   …*sleep in heavenly peace*

   …and she stepped back, a little afraid, a little bewildered, and…yes, grateful, a little grateful too. Max ran into the house. Mrs. Cavanaugh followed, but stopped before she went inside. She looked out at the woods, then up at the moon, and into the falling, drifting snow. And then she closed the door.

AN OLD SILVER THING

On a blustery, biting, blizzardly cold day last January, my 80 year old neighbor Ella Sweetlick asked me to come to her house and help take out her old Christmas tree. Funny how we think of them that way – *old* – when only two or three weeks before they were the newest, most extravagantly vibrant thing in our houses; but yes, old it was, and old it looked, old and tired and bare, standing there in her living room near the fireplace. No lights blinked and blazed. No ornaments hung from the boughs. No garlands draped and no candy canes dangled. Nothing at all distinguished this tree from its outside relatives save for a few stray threads of lifeless tinsel stranded in its branches.

I lifted it from its metal stand and dragged it toward the door. "Watch the kitty," said Ella, and I tried to block her black cat from darting out while I squeezed the old tree through the same space I tried to block, all the while trailing and spilling dried needles all over the floor. This maneuver was made infinitely easier when a draught of frozen air poured through the open door to bristle the fur on "kitty" and send him scurrying off to warmer haunts.

Through the door, I hauled the tree across her front yard and dropped it on the snow bank beside the road to be picked up by Eddie the trash guy – and really, is there a sadder sight than a January Christmas tree in the snow?

Back inside, Ella went into the kitchen to put on the kettle for tea and I began to sweep up. Near the tree stand I found a very small matchbook – at least, that's what I thought it was. I put it in my coat pocket, and didn't give it a second thought until today, nearly a year later.

It was my sheep's wool coat, which is the warmest coat I own – so warm, in fact, that it makes me wonder how sheep can stand it. Then again, I've noticed they don't put up much of a fight when the guy shows up with the shears, so maybe they can't.

Some winters I only wear it once or twice, and other winters not at all. The thermometer has to touch zero like it did on that day last January before I'd even consider wearing such a stifling garment. This morning it dropped to ten below so I threw on the coat to go out for the mail, and when I reached into my pocket in hopes of finding a stray mitten, I chanced upon that old matchbook. Looking at it again I suddenly realized it wasn't a book of matches at all – it was a book!

I opened it as best I could with the edge of my thumbnail and saw the tiniest print imaginable. Indeed, I couldn't tell

for sure if it was print at all, even after using a pair of reading glasses. I found a magnifying glass and saw that, yes, it *was* print, beautifully handwritten in spidery black ink, but my goodness, who on earth could write so small? And why do it at all if no one could read it?

Curious now, I drove to the camera store in Colebrook and asked to borrow their strongest, largest zoom lens. Using that, along with the magnifying glass and my reading glasses, I sat in a quiet corner of the store and read the story I have come to think of as *An Old Silver Thing*, though the original had no title at all.

It must have fallen out of Ella's tree last Christmas. I don't know whether you'll believe it (I had a little trouble believing it myself), but here it is all the same, just as I found it:

Twice each year we have a heart-stopping moment – can't be helped – nothing to do but hope for the best as we're taken out of our old cardboard box in early December and put back again a few weeks later. Last year we lost two silver balls. One I knew quite well, Leo Silver; spent Christmas of '73 with me on the left side of the tree, third branch down. One of the ballerinas (not my wife, thank heaven) lost her right arm in a fall. Worst of all, Mrs. Snow Scene, poor old thing, broke in our box despite her careful wrapping of tissue. You can never tell with the very old. They become so brittle.

No fear of that with me.

I am a snowman. I'm made of wood so I'm quite good

with falls, though I don't do so well when placed too close to the lights – not the bulbs' fault, snowmen suffer terribly in the heat and humidity. You see this mark on my backside? The one some think is a birthmark? Well, it's not - that comes from spending nearly two weeks backed up against a green bulb named Lois in 1983.

All in all, we ornaments have a pretty rough time. Tinsel, for example. I don't care much for tinsel, the way it mucks up the view and shines in your eyes. And then we have the class system that so humiliates us heavyset folk. I don't mind being on the lower branches, really I don't. I understand that excited children could easily break the more delicate and sensitive of us, but it is positively galling that Cecil the Rocking Horse gets to spend *every* Christmas so much higher than the rest of the wooden folk. This year he hangs only two branches down from the Angel! And yes, all right, his tail *is* made of glass, but the rest of him is solid oak. He could just as easily hang with the toy soldiers and me.

Which leads me to the Major. Ah yes, the Major…oldest of the wooden soldiers and by far the most bothersome. He is on my branch again this year. When I first saw him I thought, *If I hear one more story about the Great Cat War of 1952 I may scream and throw off my scarf. I might pluck out my carrot nose or a coal eye and throw it at him!* That is how much I simply cannot bear to listen to that old bore and his endless, "back in '52, in the war – that's the Great Cat War, 'the Big One', as its called - have I told you this? Stop me if I have. Oh, really, I have? But not *this* version, surely. So there I was, stationed on the fifth branch up from the front, when suddenly, out of the darkness, taken completely by surprise, we came under attack! Assaulted on our right flank by a feline of enormous proportions climbing the trunk," and so on and so on. No matter which "version" he tells, it is always the same endless, *endless* war story!

And now here he is, beside me on the branch, while my wife, Beverly the Ballerina, twirls six branches above. The old lady always hangs Beverly an inch or so above a lightbulb so the rising heat will catch her costume and make her spin inside her plastic star. Watching Beverly spin is one of the nicer things about hanging on a tree, but there are others. Strings of popcorn and cranberries – we all have a soft spot for those, though they are getting rarer these days. And there's my best friend Waldo the Drum. He cracks me up. And the Trumpets, Sylvia and Al. The Golden Bell sisters. Craig the Blue and Red Ball. Great bunch of kids.

And then there's Aunt Jennie-Mae. A few years ago a couple of candy canes got a little rowdy and said a few unkind words to Jennie-Mae, calling her an old silver thing or something like that. Well, let me tell you, there wasn't an ornament on the tree that didn't come down hard on those boys. Even the Angel said something, and she almost never gets involved in the goings-on of the lower branches.

The candy canes apologized but truth be told, they

were right.

Jennie-Mae *is* an old silver thing. She used to be bright red, but age has peeled her paint and the sheen of her underlying silver glass has come through.

The words on her side are still there, written with darker, stronger paint.

To my niece Ella
On Her First Christmas
Love, Aunt Jennie-Mae
Christmas, 1928

I think Aunt Jennie-Mae took the loss of Mrs. Snow Scene pretty badly. They were great friends. Used to love to chat over a nice yellow bulb; but as I said, Mrs. S. was quite elderly and frail and the poor thing didn't make it through the summer. Aunt Jennie-Mae was saddened I'm sure, but with us she remained as cheery and bright as ever.

And then *this* happened. Who on the tree could have imagined it?

A week or so ago, our owner, the old lady Ella, carefully lifted us from our boxes and put us on the tree as always, and we hung on our assigned branches, either satisfied or complaining, depending on our position and neighbors.

Last night was Christmas Eve and it was a lovely evening. Ella, her daughters, sons-in-law, grandchildren and lots of grandnieces and nephews had all gone to bed and we were free to do as we pleased. The night began normally enough. Beverly and I went over to the fourth branch to visit with the Trumpets. Waldo came with us, of course. Sylvia Trumpet was her usual charming self, and Al was a perfect host, serving popcorn and cranberries by the yard. The Bell sisters stopped by and they all, Bells, Trumpets and Drum, joined in a lovely rendition of "Oh Holy Night". They were about to start in on Waldo's favorite song (and surely you can guess which one it is) when a bugle sounded from somewhere below.

That wasn't unusual. The soldiers often gather on Christmas Eve to play cards and swap stories, and sometimes play carols on their bugles, especially after they have gotten into the eggnog. But this wasn't a carol. It sounded more like an alarm, or a call to arms.

I didn't know what to do. I only came on board in 1968 and had never experienced anything like this. The lights began to blink – even the older ones who would never dream of blinking began to flash as bright and quick as the young. The glass balls chattered nervously amongst themselves and moved instinctively toward the top of the tree while those few soldiers who'd strayed up to flirt with the ballerinas raced downward, drawn by the bugle's call.

"What's happening, Snow?" Beverly asked, but I couldn't answer. I was as confused as anyone. I looked to the top of the tree, hoping the Angel might have an answer, but she did not move or say a word. She watched the goings-on below with dark eyes, calm and silent.

The candy canes raced to the back of the tree, babbling like ninnies.

And then came the Major, blustering through the mayhem:

99

"Up! Up, everybody!" he shouted. "You there - you Snowmen, step back! Glass and Porcelain first!"

Panic took hold. The tree swarmed with blinking, moving shapes; wooden ornaments heading down, fragile glass struggling upward, and overall, the Major's booming voice: "Stand firm, chaps! Stand firm!"

And then I saw it. We *all* saw it, looming out of the shadows, a great hulking beast unlike anything I had ever seen. It came steady and silent through the gloom below, its glittering eyes fixed upon us.

"Oh, what is it, what is it?" cried Beverly, and Al Trumpet (a former military reservist) said, "I'd better join the others down there."

"I'm going too," said Sylvia, but Al wouldn't hear of it. "Too bad," she snapped, and tightened her strap. Al smiled and the two brave trumpets started down. One of the Golden Bell sisters began to cry. "Now, now," the other said, and before the first could respond, there came a voice from above, seemingly as an echo. "Now, now," it said, and everyone on the top third of the tree looked up.

It was the old silver girl herself, Aunt Jennie-Mae. She hung from her high, protected branch below the Angel, surveying all below. "Don't be afraid," she tried to say to a trembling group of glass ornaments, but a dreadful yowl overpowered her words.

The Thing attacked!

Solid black it was, with blazing eyes. All muscle and fur and teeth and claws, an unholy beast risen from a nightmare. A great paw emerged from the darkness and struck Louis the Reindeer on the lowest branch. His hook

snapped and he shrieked as he plummeted down upon the presents below.

It leaped! Tinsel tore away, tangled in its claws.

"Sally forth, men!" the Major commanded. "Into the breach!"

Soldiers, trumpets and drums, and a cannon decorated with holly rushed in. The Thing met them with a fury of snarls and slashing claws. Several brave soldiers fell beneath the onslaught. "Charge!" cried the Major. A second battalion marched forward. The Major rushed toward the back of the tree and grabbed Cecil the Rocking Horse by his reins. "Hold the line men!" he cried as he stormed to the head of the branch, but it was too late.

The Thing fought through our defensive line and reached the center of the tree, the very heart of our operations. Up it went, clawing at the trunk. Bells rang, candy canes screeched, trumpets blared, but on it came.

A small green ball fell with a cry.

Beverly screamed as the Thing tore past, digging its razor claws into the bark as higher and higher it climbed.

"Great Scott!" cried the Major. "It's heading for Jennie-Mae!"

The old boy came into his own then. He leaped upon a startled Cecil and led the charge of the wooden brigade up over the branches and spruce needles. A swarm of soldiers, snowmen and reindeer followed, all wielding icicle spears and bared antlers, and all intent upon stopping the dreadful enemy, which even then bore in upon the uppermost branches.

It soon became clear that we were about to face the very thing that most strikes terror into the hearts of even the firmest ornaments - a tipped tree!

Smaller boughs bent under the weight of the Beast. The tree wobbled and leaned. The candy canes shrieked. "We're gonna tip! We're gonna tip!"

"Silence there, you canes!" the Major bellowed. "All nonessential personnel to the rear! *Now!*" Those ornaments not involved in the battle swept around to the back. The tree tilted upright again. "Onward men!" the Major cried. "Reindeer - take the left flank. You there! Snowman! Move!"

I tried, but I'm a snowman! I don't have feet. I was out of breath just trying to climb from branch to branch. How could I stand up against something so nimble and powerful?

The Thing reached out. It swiped the air. A branch

103

bent and a great cry rose up as Aunt Jennie-Mae's hook slid toward the end of the branch.

"Do something!" Beverly shouted, but what could I do? I'm just a snowman! And so, with my trembling heart stopped and breath caught in my wooden chest, I stared in helpless dread as Aunt Jennie-Mae reached the end of her branch...and fell, an endless fall of old silver, streaking down, brushing past the other branches and landing on the floor with a single, crisp, resounding *crack*.

A voice called from the top of the stairs, our owner's voice, the old lady Ella. "Bandit? What are you doing down there?" The Thing froze, listening - "Here, kitty, come upstairs now," – and then scampered backward down the trunk and dropped to the floor. It glanced back at us, its eyes shining with mischief; and quick as a flash, it lifted its tail straight up like a victorious black battle flag and darted from the room.

We did not move.

Small bits of glass littered the floor.

We did not say a word. No one knew what to say, but presently there came a soft flutter of wings, and there she was, the Angel, hovering before us, radiant and aglow.

"*Do not be afraid,*" she said, echoing Aunt Jennie-Mae's own words. "*Old silver passes and new silver rises, and so it has been since first I sang above a lowly manger. Do not be afraid.*"

That was all she said. Words, meaningless in our grief. The tree would never be the same. It *could* never be the same, we were certain of it. We felt that a chord had broken, as if we'd lost the center from which we radiated like multi-colored spokes; and the feelings remained well into morning when the old lady came downstairs holding the dreadful Beast in her arms.

She stopped at the foot of the stairs.

"Oh no," she whispered and lowered her arms. The Thing dropped but landed on its feet with a soft thud. The old lady stood before us, staring at the floor. "Oh no," she said again. That was all she said as she got a dustpan and whisk broom from the kitchen and swept the last remaining fragments of her childhood's Christmas away forever.

I would have stopped here, with only this sad tale as this year's Christmas event, but the old woman did not stop.

She reached down into the assembled gifts and pulled one out.

She unwrapped it, all alone before the tree, and held it

up before the brilliance of the lights.

It was a glass ball, shiny and red, upon which she had painted:

To my great-niece Mary
On her first Christmas.
Love Aunt Ella
Christmas, 2009

I don't know what to say about all this. Old silver and new, the Angel's words, memories of Aunt Jennie-Mae...I don't know what it all means.

What I *do* know is this: the Major is back on the branch beside me and he has started in again. "Let me tell you about the Great Cat War II, 'the *Really* Big One.'"

TOBIAS

IN THE DONKEY BARN

Tiny Mickens is the least tiniest man in town. He is exceeded in girth and weight only by his draft horse Peablossom and his wife, Madge, who must weigh in at...well, no. Gentlemanly discretion prevents me from hazarding a guess (though, by way of illustration, I will quote a mutual friend who estimates the dimensions of her nether parts as roughly, "two axe handles across").

Some of you may already know Peablossom, as he is the only true celebrity in our town, having won the blue ribbon two years in a row in the horse-pulling contest at the Lancaster Fair.

He lives in the largest stall in the Mickens donkey barn. All the other inhabitants, seven in all, are the smallest, cutest donkeys imaginable. Now donkeys, as a rule, are considered fairly useless, at least up here in the North Woods. They can't haul a plow or timber sledges like

Peablossom can. They don't give milk anyone wants to put in their tea. They don't do much of anything beyond standing around, flicking their ears and staring at nothing, but Tiny and Madge are devoted to their little herd. They used to lease the animals out to local towns to raise funds by playing donkey basketball, but the sight of their neighbors astride the donkeys, kicking their sides and pulling their ears, proved too much for the kindhearted Mickenses', and they retired them all.

Every winter, I receive an invitation that reads like this:

*Tiny and Madge Mickens cordially invite you to join
Topaz, Romero, Pebble, Tucker, Fiona, Licorice, Hollie
and their elder brother Peablossom,
in the Donkey Barn
for an evening of Hot Mulled Cider and Song,
And the Tale of the Donkey, Tobias, as retold by Madge
Mickens*

The party always takes place on a Friday night in mid-December, and always in the donkey barn, snug and warm with a fire blazing in that big Franklin stove they have. The barn itself is cleared of tools and tractor parts, the floors scrubbed clean, and the walls and lofts bright with colored lantern light. The normally pungent livestock smells are banished, forced into exile by fresh, woodsy garlands of spruce and pine, and the ripe-apple scent of hot cider laced with orange peel, cloves, and cinnamon. Candlelight glistens on glazed turkeys and quivers deep and red on the surface of Madge's homemade cranberry sauce. Bottles clank, jars clink, piles and stacks of sweet and savory dishes too numerous to name jostle and vie for position on the tabletop, and dietary rules and restrictions are thrown aside as everyone fills their bowl to the brim and piles their plate high and tottering. Cheerful indulgence reigns.

The donkeys love it too, especially the baskets of carrots that hang from each stall. Each one wears a garland of red or green around its neck, and a green elf hat perched between its long ears, while Peablossom wears a red furred Santa's hat between his.

Lively carols scratch out from an ancient turntable that still plays 45's of Bing Crosby and Perry Como and we all sit on bales of hay, or dangle our legs from the loft, and eat and sing and laugh and tell jokes, or pat the donkeys and feed them sugar and candy canes, or watch the younger girls braid ribbons into Peablossom's mane; but at some point, as though heralded by an unseen chime, all noise and movement settles down (but for the occasional snort or stamp from the stalls) and Madge Mickens, resplendent in newly pressed overalls and a blouse nearly as red as her cheeks, steps into the middle of the barn. She no longer introduces herself or the story, since most of us have heard it year after year. She begins by saying one tiny word, simply:

TOBIAS

"A small donkey lived in a small barn behind a middling-sized boarding house in a fairly large town. His name was Tobias. He was gray, he was small, and he didn't mind being called a donkey, though his long ears turned red whenever anyone referred to him as an 'ass'."

Tittering escapes from somewhere near the stalls behind Madge. "Shush," someone says from the hayloft, and "Quiet!" whispers another someone balanced on the door of a donkey stall. She continues: "Tobias once had a lovely disposition. He was a gentle creature who gladly gave children rides and willingly carried bundles of kindling or hay or anything else that could be loaded onto his back; and he did all this without a single hee-hawing complaint. All that changed however, when he was sold to the owner of the boarding house, Ezekiel Slagg."

Boos and hisses from the hay loft!

"That's right," Madge says. "He was a great, cruel brute with a thick neck nearly hidden by a great ginger-colored beard, and to say he mistreated Tobias is, at best, an understatement.

"It wasn't enough to haul wood and water all day, no! Poor Tobias felt the whip across his back with every misstep, and at night, when he limped into his stall, what was there for him? Grain?"

"No!" call the party guests.

"Oats?" Madge asks.

"No!"

"Carrots or even a stale old radish?"

"No!"

"Was there enough straw to lie down upon?"

"No, no, no!" the guests cry and stomp their feet.

"No, there was not!" Madge says in loud agreement. "Nothing but a few strands of hay to eat. It was the same for all of them: Muriel the cow, and the sheep, Rodney and Emily. No one ever had enough to eat, and yet they did not understand that the constant, gnawing in their bellies was all that unusual. They did not realize that other barnyard animals were treated better and never knew such pain or hunger. Like all animals, and most children, they simply thought, This is how it is, and left it at that.

"One night Ezekiel Slagg drove Tobias into the barn with a sharp crack of the whip - nothing unusual, of course - but this time, Tobias jumped and his hoof came up quite unexpectedly to strike the big man a little below the knee. 'Why, you little devil!' he yelled, and brought the whip down again and again. Tobias tried to escape but couldn't. The barn, the stalls, the walls – he couldn't turn, he couldn't run. Mr. Slagg harried him, slashing him with the whip, over and over. 'I should have killed you for meat!' the horrible man yelled, and Tobias kicked his back legs and brayed and did all he could to escape the lash.

"His hooves hit the wall – bang!

"Crack went the wood!

"His hind legs went up again – bang!

"Crack again, this time of the whip, and Tobias kicked. Bang! Hooves – bang, bang, bang - and through! Boards broke, wood splintered, a hole opened and the little donkey fled from the barn!

"Ezekiel Slagg lowered the whip, and stood there, out of breath, his fury simmering. In the stunned silence that followed he heard nothing but the *cree-craw, cree-craw* of a broken board swinging back and forth from a rusty nail, and in the distance, the soft *clippety-clippety-clippety* of hooves racing away from him, growing fainter, softer, and then… gone.

"Free! Tobias' heart surged as he ran through the lonely streets. He wished he could be happy too, but he couldn't, for he knew that men were evil, men were cruel, and the only chance he had for real happiness was to leave them far behind. Otherwise, he would always be a slave, a beast of burden in a life of endless drudgery, with nothing of joy, nothing of the sweet thing, the donkey thing, the thing about being gray and small and not wanting much beyond a cool summer day and a carrot. None of that could happen, not with men, and so he ran. Stars shimmered above, but he didn't notice them. He did not want to notice them - not the shimmering stars, nor the sparkling windows in the gradually fading town. He wanted only to escape – *Never again!* he thought. *I will never again have anything to do with them. I once was innocent. I kicked up my hooves and brayed with happiness, but that is all gone now. They have whipped it out of me. I have nothing left to give, and so I run. I run. I run.*

"The lights of town faded and darkness fell, marred only by the stars shining like pinpricks through a black shroud; and it was only then, in the deep stillness, that the small donkey dared slow down. They were far behind him then, men, and nothing lay before him but wide open road and sky and stars, and so he slowed and slowed - *clip-clop, clip-clop* - and he limped and slowed beneath the stars.

"He passed over a rise and – 'Look!' he heard. 'Look!

See what comes over the hill!'

"Someone ran to him through the darkness. Before Tobias could react, a man grabbed him by the halter. Tobias reared back and tried to escape, but the man spoke to him gently, 'There now, sweet donkey… there now. Please carry her.'

"Tobias pulled back. The halter slipped from the man's hand. 'Please,' he whispered. 'Please…'

"Tobias hesitated. *Why should I?* he thought. *Your kind has whipped and beaten me until I do not know what I am anymore.*

"The man caught him by the halter again and gently pulled his head down and to the side. 'Look,' he whispered, turning Tobias' head to the side of the road.

"A woman sat beneath a leafless tree, covered by shadow, hidden from the stars. There was something different about her. Tobias could see that, even through the shadows. He had seen hundreds of women before, but never one like this.

"He shook his head. *'No!'* he thought, *'They are all alike, they hate and they hurt,'* and he pulled away again.

"The man released the halter but followed as the donkey backed up the small hill. 'Please,' he said, and pointed up into the sky without taking his eyes off Tobias. 'Please,' he said again. 'I need you. Please…'

"Tobias stopped. He stared at the man. He didn't want

to – men were cruel – but he couldn't help it. He looked up to where the man pointed and saw…something – a brightness in the sky, and he gave himself up.

"His back had been cruelly whipped, but he allowed the woman to ride upon it.

"They needed help but the little donkey knew of no place to bring them except the town from which he had made his escape, and there he went – *clip-clop, clip-clop* -

though he knew the journey back would deliver him once more into bondage.

"*Clip-clop, clip-clop*…The slow journey back into town, through the lonely streets, past windows lit with oil lamps… *Clip-clop, clip-clop*…through silence, silence all around, until they came to the door.

"Once there, Tobias held back in the shadows while the man knocked upon the door of the very boardinghouse that had caused him so much pain. He retreated farther and trembled beneath the burden of the woman when Mr. Slagg appeared, still riled with fury brought on by his swollen knee. 'No!' he exploded. 'No! You cannot get a room here! I don't care where you go, but you cannot stay here!'

"He slammed the door.

"The man suggested they try to find another boarding house but – 'No,' the woman said, her voice jagged and urgent. She clutched her stomach and said, 'Now…'

"The man looked around, frantic. He ran to Mr. Slagg's front door, about to knock again and plead for mercy, but Tobias slammed his foot down upon the cobblestones. The man turned, startled. Tobias tossed his head and carried the stricken woman around the side of the boarding house. The man followed as the donkey moved through the back courtyard into the small barn he knew so well. Tobias nodded to the cow and the sheep, and stopped at the far end of the barn, beside the manger.

"He turned away as the woman, laying in the hay on the floor of the stable with her husband beside her, and with the cows and sheep and donkey in attendance, brought new life into the world, there in the lowly barn.

"A star brightened above, the same one Tobias had

seen earlier when the man had pointed to the sky. Shepherds from the fields saw and followed it into the silent streets. Others came bearing gifts – shepherds and kings, the foolish and the wise, the high-born and the low, all following the light of the star, and the barn filled. The manger was surrounded by gifts, and soon became so crowded with shepherds and wise men and the cow and sheep that Tobias was forced out into the street.

"It was just as well. He was only a little donkey. He didn't matter.

"And yet…through the throng, through the gold and frankincense and myrrh, through the flowing robes of brocade and silk and the tattered threadbare garments of the shepherds and even through the cotton robe of Mr. Slagg who bent over the baby and cooed and smiled as though it was his own child, through all this, the mother caught sight of a small patch of gray fur.

"She lifted her hand.

"The great star glittered and Tobias shuddered. Something came over him, a feeling that someone was reaching out for him. He turned to look into the stable and everyone - the shepherds, the wise men and even Mr. Slagg - parted, and he, Tobias the donkey, stared across the barn at the mother and her child.

"She couldn't possibly be looking at him – *Not me!* he thought, *Not a donkey, not a little donkey* - but she held her hand out to him.

"Tobias' ears turned red. He moved through the gathered men, slowly – *clip-clop, clip-clop* – and they stared at him. Some had carried myrrh and frankincense. Some had carried gold. What had he brought? What had he carried?

"*Clip-clop, clip-clop*, slow across the barn, *This isn't right, I'm only a donkey. Clip-clop, clip-clop.*

"He stopped before the mother, Mary. She touched him. She ran her fingers down his muzzle to his soft mouth, and turned toward the manger.

"Tobias looked at the baby and there he saw all that the star had promised.

"Now, don't holler at me," says Madge Mickens. "I'm only the story teller. I know you want to hear that Tobias kicked Mr. Slagg in the slats, thereby redeeming all of donkeydom, but the truth is, it didn't happen. It couldn't. The owner of the boarding house fell under the spell of the manger, the same as everyone else, and would never be the same. He would never treat Tobias badly again.

"And Tobias would never be the same either. *No one* would be the same, ever again. And so now, look at it: the Nativity scene over there beside Peablossom's stall. Look at those small plaster figures of Mary and Joseph, and the baby in the manger. Who is that with them? He is small and grey. His name is Tobias, and they say that he carried them there."

JENNY TRALEE
AND THE GRANDIOSE MOOSE

Jenny Tralee in her snowsuit and scarf
And her mittens and snowboots went out for a laugh.*
She took her red sled up onto Puckerbrush Hill
With Melissa and Jackson and Michael and Jill.

There, until sunset, they glided and slid.
Up and down, up and down again - that's all they did
Until night came upon them on Puckerbrush Hill
Under skies cold and clear, under stars bright and still.

Jenny Tralee started home in the dark,
Through the field at the left of the new trailer park,
Past the houses on Muffinlee Road where she said
"What on earth is that thing that I see up ahead?"

Christmas lights danced and they upped and they downed
And they thrashed and they darted around and around,
And they should have – they didn't – but *should* have come loose,
For the lights had entangled a ten-foot-tall moose.

His antlers were caught in the holiday lights,
(And truly, this was the most dazzling of sights,)
And the moose, in all truth, did not know what the heck
All those blinky things were 'round his muzzle and neck.

---

*Yes it *does* rhyme, - if you are from New England. Try starting over
saying it this way:
> "Jenny Tralee in her snowsuit and scaaahf
>
> And her mittens and snowboots went out for a laaaugh"

123

"Tell me," he snorted, "what's this on my head?"
And Jenny Tralee held her red sled and said,
"Oh dear Sir, you are lit from your antler to hoof,
By the lights you tore off Mrs. Loonylock's roof!"

The brute rather liked how he looked in the glow;
The reflection he saw in the parlor window.
"If I stroll so festooned through the pine and the spruce,
I shall be the most widely admired of moose!"

Jenny Tralee stepped up close, dropped her sled
And she frowned when the ten-foot-tall tangled moose said,
"With my red, blue and gold blinky bright outerwear,
As they say in Quebec, Je suis *trés* debonair!

I am magnificent! Look what *I've* done!
I am simply the finest moose under the sun!"
"Oh but no, Mr. Moose," chimed in Jenny Tralee,
"For you must give some credit to 'lectricity."

The moose brushed her off and continued to preen,
"I shall *not* share the credit with someone unseen!"
And he snorted and shuffled, and turned round about
Then he took a step forward and promptly - went out.

"What's this?" he gasped. "Where's my grandeur and glow?
Where's my splendid reflection in yonder window?
All my effort has vanished, and now look at me,
I am nothing! I'm common! I'm ordinary!"

"Oh, no!" Jenny said, "you're terribly wrong,
You are furry and lovely, and noble and strong!
And, Sir, this is what happened" - she held up the cord.
"It was this that you broke, it was this you ignored.

The Christmas Mink

Some say moose look goofy, but what do they know?
Have they ever seen one so up close in the snow?
Those lights added nothing – oh, don't be dismayed
You are perfect and lovely the way you were made."

"Untangle me, please," said the satisfied moose
And the girl whispered low as she shook the bulbs loose,
"I wish you the merriest Holiday, I do,"
And he nuzzled her cheek and he said, "Same to you."

Jenny Tralee wandered off to her home,
And the moose wandered off to wherever moose roam,
And the far away stars draped them both in a light,
That was constant, unfailingly steady and bright.

Finding Frostwin
A Misadventure Of The Elves,
Jeremiah Blizzard And Arthur Sleet

I was in the paint shop, putting the finishing touches on a rocking horse's bridle and humming cheery yuletide tunes, when the screechy loudspeaker jarred me from my reverie with the following words: "Blizzard to the office! Jeremiah Blizzard to the office!"

Oh, now what? I wondered, which is a path down whose well-trodden ways my thoughts often meander since the day my fortunes were tied to my fellow elf, Arthur Sleet. He may have annoyed someone or broken something, and somehow – *somehow* – conjured a way to drag me into it; and so I climbed the office stairs with a heavy heart and that eternal question upon my lips: *Oh, now what?*

I entered the office and, to my surprise, the first thing I saw was the big, burly man himself, our esteemed leader, S. Clause seated at a desk opposite Wenceslas, the paint shop foreman (Mr. Claus rarely comes to the paint shop, some say because he dislikes the smell of turpentine, though it's more likely he simply forgets where it is).

"There you are!" Santa cried in a merry voice loud enough to shatter crystal and wake the dead. His Secret Service detail, alarmed by the sound, burst into the office from the side hall, wearing their usual identical dark green suits, dark glasses, form-fitting pointy ear pieces, and shiny black patent-leather curly toed shoes. Apparently mistaking my startled expression of surprise for that of a blood-crazed assassin, they flew across the room, piled onto me, pinned me to the floor, and elf-handled me in a most abusive way before Santa waved them off with a jolly laugh reminiscent of a foghorn. "I admire your enthusiasm, lads, but this – Ha- *hoooo* – this one is harmless." The bodyguards climbed off me and moved to the far side of the room where they stood with arms folded, grim and watchful. "Hope they haven't hurt you," Santa boomed while I, lying upon the floor at his feet, set about untangling my arms from behind my back and lifting my face from the floorboards.

"Oh, no doubt they have," I said, having long ago given up on the idea of escaping completely unscathed from anything. After catching sight of a scowl across the room, I quickly added, "But nothing serious. A scratch or two; possibly a slight dislocation…mere trifles."

"And you - " He interrupted himself with another inexplicable foghorn blast. "Ha-ha-*hoooo!* And you have recovered from that unfortunate tumble from the sleigh, have you?"

"I have, Sir, yes," I said, picking myself up from the floor and dusting myself off, "and I thank you for asking. Only a slight limp, and the bit

131

with the eyes unable to blink at the same time. And the teeth still jiggling about a bit. But apart from that, I am fit as a fiddle."

"Happy to hear it!" he said, and slapped me on the back with such force and velocity that one of those selfsame jiggling teeth flew from mouth and hit the far office window with a *crack*, which made Santa laugh so hard he began to cough. No one offered him any water or made a move to help him, but that seemed not to matter in the least. "No, no, I'm fine, I'm fine!" he said, waving away absolutely no one. "No really, don't trouble yourselves, I'm fine, I'm *fine*!"

I looked at Wenceslas. He looked at me, and then shrugged his shoulders. "So yes," said Santa, recovering. "So…so, yes. Is that so! You really *have* been to Northern Siberia, have you?"

I looked around, waiting for the person addressed to answer, and – as all stood gazing placidly at me – I realized that *I* must be that person. "Oh…well, yes, I have, yes," I stammered, a bit confused as I did not recall him nor anyone else broaching the subject of Northern Siberia in the first place.

"Marvelous!" he boomed. "And I'm quite certain you found it a most interesting place. Yes, yes, most interesting indeed. The cold, the mesmerizing darkness, the indigenous hordes whose quaint Slavic folkways so enchant; yes, yes, I have always maintained – *and do to this day* – that there is simply no place quite so interesting as…"

A look as blank as the endless tundra crossed his face.

"Northern Siberia?" I offered.

"Ah, yes!" he said, and slapped his knee. "Yes, yes, Northern Siberia! Dreadful place. Cold. Dark. Utterly uninteresting. Why *anyone* would go there is a mystery quite beyond my comprehension."

"Sooty too," I ventured.

"What is?"

"Northern Siberia."

"Is it? How interesting."

"Terribly sooty," I said. "All those smokestacks."

"Ah, yes, the smoky sootstacks," he said gravely. "Why anyone would venture there is a mystery. Still, I'm sure you will have a marvelous time!"

I stared, and though I said nothing, Santa looked at me and asked, "Yes?"

"You said I'll have a wonderful time in Northern Siberia."

"Did I? Wonder why. Never known anyone to have a wonderful time in that ghastly place."

Wenceslas cleared his throat and leaned toward Santa. "Frostwin, sir."

Santa slapped the desk top and laughed again, as jolly as could be. "Of course, of course!" he cried. "How could I forget? Sometimes I wonder how I…" He trailed off, chuckling to himself before settling down to gaze at me with a blank stare. "And we were talking about…?"

"Frostwin, sir," Wenceslas said, staring at the ceiling. "We were talking about Frostwin. He's missing."

"Oh, that's *right*, that's right," said Santa. "Frostwin!"

"Missing?" I asked, quite aghast at the idea. No wonder the paint shop had been so quiet of late, so restful and serene.

"Indeed, yes," Santa said. "Can't find a single flake of him. Normally I wouldn't mind. In fact, I've rather warmed to the idea of never seeing Frostwin again, but we have a large gathering of Albanian orphans scheduled for a visit, and they particularly asked to see him."

"To see *him*?" I asked, wondering what could possibly be running through their little parentless minds.

"Yes, *him*," Santa said with something of a shudder. "Apparently that song – you know the one I mean – is unaccountably popular in Albania. You know, the one that goes like...oh, how does it go again? Oh, yes, it goes something like this: 'Frosty the la-la, was a something-something-soul. With a la-dee-da, and a dum-dum-dum and two something-something-coal...'"

Now about that song so beloved in orphanages throughout Albania. Like nearly every other song about our lives at the North Pole, it's almost entirely wrong from start to finish. Most of them are. Rudolph the Red-Nosed Reindeer, for instance, has absolutely no interest in reindeer games and even less interest in flying around in the fog. He would much rather spend his days in bed, snuggled under the covers with his nose lit up, reading *The Adventures of Spotty the Wonder-Fawn*. As for Frosty the Snowman...well, *everything* about that song is wrong, wrong, wrong. Even the name is wrong. It is not Frosty. It is Frostwin T. Bhoggan, and the only time he's within striking distance of being considered a "jolly, happy soul" is when he's gotten into the rum punch. Even then, he's rather more tiresome than joyful. He doesn't smoke a corncob pipe. He smokes thick, terribly smelly cigars. His nose is not a button; it's a carrot. And yes, all right, fine – yes, he *does* have two eyes made out of coal, but that, my friends, is the only shred of genuine truth in the song.

Just picture it, won't you? "Down to the village with a

broomstick in his hand, running here and there all around the square saying, 'catch me if you can!'" How annoying is *that*? No one in their right mind wants a clumsy oaf of a snowman snockered on rum punch running around *anywhere*, especially swinging a broomstick, knocking people's hats off and vandalizing property. And if you think Frostwin "only paused a moment" when that cop yelled at him, you are sorely mistaken. No, he jumped into a sleigh, drove it the wrong way down Sugardrop Street and straight through the front showcase window of Tigglewags Used Ornaments. Oh yes, what a jolly happy soul! What a peach!

And now the assignment to find him and bring him back had fallen to me. "How am I to do this?" I asked. By using the same old sleigh and elderly reindeer that had put me in the Elf Ward for six months. "Will I be going alone?" I asked warily, and my heart quivered like a bowl of holiday gelatin in anticipation of Santa's answer.

"Alone?" he said. "Certainly not, my dear boy, no! I would never ask such a thing of you nor, for that matter, any other elf in my employ. There is another well-acquainted with your destination, and with him you shall go. His name is…" He squinted.

"Sleet?" I inquired with a meek, fearful squeak.

"The very same!" he cried and my heart sank like an ill-fated ocean liner, with little deck chairs tumbling and crashing throughout my arteries and veins. "Arthur Sleet! He knows Northern Siberia better than anyone."

"But why Northern Siberia?" I asked. "How do we know Frostwin went there?"

"Why it's very simple," said Santa, and from the blank

look rising in his eyes, I knew he hadn't a clue.

"Because he told us," said Wenceslas from the side of his mouth.

Santa roared with laughter and slapped his knee with such force that one might have supposed that someone had said something funny. "Ha-ha-*hoooo*! That's right, that's *right*!" he bellowed, and he took off his furred hat and withdrew a yellow piece of paper from inside. "And here is the very telegram by which he did so."

He handed it to me.

DEAR SANTA…STOP…
IN NORTHERN SIBERIA…STOP…
CATCH ME IF YOU CAN…STOP…FROSTWIN.

When I finished, Santa once again roared with laughter, this time with tears rolling down his cheeks. No one else laughed. The bodyguards never cracked a smile. Wenceslas and I looked at each other, wondering what on earth could possibly be that funny. "I trust," Santa said, trying to catch his breath, "I trust you will do as I ask."

I glanced at the Secret Service, presumably glaring at me from behind their dark glasses.

"I suppose I must," I whispered.

Santa's laugh died at once and he grabbed me by the shoulders with such force that my head snapped back. "Indeed you must," he said, and shook me so hard that I heard something rattle in my skull. "For the sake of the Albanian orphanhood, you *must* find him!"

I trudged forlorn and miserable through the village, searching for Artie and bemoaning my fate. I found him and our team of doddering old reindeer in the sleigh wash.

He had taken them there in the vain hope of making them presentable for the flight.

"Greetings, Jerry!" he called from the back of that ramshackle old horror of a sleigh. He wore the largest pair of earmuffs I had ever seen, made of white fur. The elderly reindeer stood in front of the sleigh, each one lathered in suds. Two elves worked them over with soap and buckets of warm water.

The sleigh tilted and creaked when I climbed in beside him. "What have you gotten me into?" I asked.

Artie squinted and cocked his head. "Huh?"

I lifted one of the earmuffs. "What have you - ow!" Something bit my finger. "What in the world...?" I leaned back, startled to see that what I'd thought were earmuffs were actually two white rabbits suspended in a leather harness, one dangling on each side of Artie's head and both glaring furiously at me with their sinister, beady black eyes. Their whiskers and upper lips rose up and down in a series of silent, yet 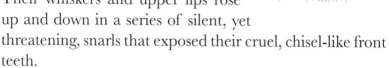 threatening, snarls that exposed their cruel, chisel-like front teeth.

"Snow bunnies!" Artie explained. "You know how oversized my ears are – always difficult to cover, always cold, so I hit upon this as a remedy. They're awfully warm. Want to try?"

As ridiculous as they appeared, I had to admit that, yes, they did look warm, so I gave it a go. I took off my elf hat and draped the harness over my head, careful to place the two snow bunnies over my ears. "Why, yes," I said, "quite toasty," and whether it was the sound of my voice or the unusual pointiness of my ears remains unclear, but something startled those rabbits into a frenzy. They began to kick with their back legs and squealed and bit with their cruel, chisel-like teeth, and for the life of me, I couldn't untangle their harness from of my head. "Help!" I cried.

Artie's elf training always kicks in when he becomes nervous or flustered, which causes him to say "hee-hee" or "ho-ho" at the least appropriate times – and this was one such time. "Hee-*heeee!*" he cried, and tried to grab the frenzied rabbits. They eluded his grasp. "Hold…ho-ho-ho! Hold still!"

"Get them off, get them off!" The ghastly rabbits continued to kick with the same vicious determination they brought to digging a burrow, which rendered a successful attempt to follow Artie's advice to 'hold still' remote at best. "Someone shoot them!" I howled. The snow bunnies screeched and howled and made all sorts of harrowing noises not often heard in a rabbit hutch. "Artie, do something! Get them *off* me!"

He suddenly stopped with the hee-heeing and held his hands up before them, palms outward. "Silence, my bunnies," he intoned in a calm, restful voice, like a spiritual guru in pointy shoes. "Breathe deeply and freely. Let go of your cares. That's it, that's it. Breathe, little bunnies. Be still and serene." With each soothing word, the demons gave up the battle bit by bit, and by the time he said, "Be tranquil my fluffies," they drooped in their harness and hung limp over my ears. He carefully removed the infernal contraption and put it back on his own head. "See?" he said with a broad grin. "They respond to kindness."

The rabbits glared at me.

"Why," I asked, dabbing at the blood on my face, "why is *everything* so difficult when I'm with you?"

Once again we had to use the oldest sleigh still in service and the same elderly reindeer team that had nearly killed us a mere twelve months before. One would have thought that one or two of the old fellows would have reached the end of their tether and hastened off to the great tundra in the sky, but no – there they were, all eight of them, another year older, with a few less teeth and more broken antlers, and most as deaf and some as blind as a fence post. One the latter was Gonner, great-grandfather to that celebrity of the pasture, Donner. Because of this, Artie had put him in the lead. It didn't matter that he couldn't see his hoof in front of his face.

"Fly!" Artie yelled, and the two startled sleigh washers dropped their buckets and leaped out of the way, the way they always did for those snorting, vibrant teams that leaped without hesitation and tore through the open door of the sleigh wash. But this time, they leaped for naught. No one moved. Nothing happened. "Fly!" Artie yelled again.

"What?" Gonner asked.

"Fly! On! Go! Sail proudly into the clouds, my noble steeds!"

The reindeer all turned their heads at once to look at him, puzzled. The two sleigh washers quickly turned away, though I still heard their stifled, through-the-nose laughter. I sighed and rolled my eyes. Turning to the washers, now red-faced and doing everything they could not to look at each other, I said, "Kindly lead us out of here, won't you? And when we get outside, you might want to give the 'noble steeds' a sharp slap to get us going."

This they did, and after the usual collisions with every spruce and pine tree that had the misfortune to find itself in our path, we lifted rough and bouncy into the clouds, and on we went, silently fleeting through the night. We soared over vast and silent ice floes, empty of all things but white, and over the tundra where the arctic foxes called and sang, and then came the evergreen forests stretching on and on below us.

I sat in the back. Artie drove, which thankfully meant I did not have to endure the stares of the snowbunnies. I saw only their fluffy tails and their ears flowing straight back in the wind. I sat back with my hands clasped behind my head and breathed in the pine-scented air. *Well, this is quite pleasant*, I thought. *Lovely view. Lovely moon. Lovely not to be subjected to the snarling visages of those wretched rabbits, the villains. Try your tricks on me again, mateys, and I'll drop you overboard to the foxes.* And so, with my mind occupied by such pleasantries, I whiled away the time, content and even happy; but then the reality of our mission intruded to banish all joy.

Frostwin. My heart sank. The very thought of him coagulated what little mirth remained. Below us lay immense fields of evergreens, reaching from horizon to horizon without a single clearing or tiny light to break their sinister darkness. "How on earth are we to find that abominable snowman in all of this?" I asked in despair.

"Oh, it's easy!" Artie said in a cheerful voice, though I don't know how he heard me considering what lay upon his ears. "I know where to look."

"In all this?" I asked, and glanced down once more.

"What?" He lifted one of the rabbits from his ears.

"In all this?" I asked again. "You know where to find

him in all this?"

"Of course not. You know Frostwin. Bored rigid in a place like this, nothing but trees and more trees. Perhaps an occasional wolverine, for contrast. No, he prefers something far more lively, and I know exactly where it is. The Blue Icicle. Sooner or later, he always ends up there."

"The Blue Icicle?" I had never heard of it.

"The Blue Icicle Pub and Pool Hall. Lively place; very popular with the snowmen. Pool tables. Honky-tonk piano. Enormous frozen cocktails. And then there's the barmaid, Carla. Big ol' snowmaid, with two thin little sticks for arms and the prettiest icicle for a nose, all smooth and clear and sharp."

I squinted at his back. "How is it that I don't know her?" No answer. I shrugged my shoulders and tried to let the question pass without further comment, but I couldn't. Before the Workelf Compensation Board assigned me to the toy barn, I had spent years in the coalmines with Artie, scrounging for the stray pieces of coal Santa required for the ever-increasing numbers of VBKs. We had few breaks, and even fewer days off. Never had any fun. So how was it Artie happened to know so much about a pool hall?

Not daring to touch his earmuffs, I tapped him on the back. This startled him and he swung around so quickly that the two snow bunnies lifted up and twirled around twice, straight out at the ends of their tethers, like a slow-moving propeller atop his head. "Yes?" he asked. The bunnies slowed and came to a stop, once more covering his ears.

"How do you know Carla? And how do you know the Blue Icicle Pub?"

"Oh," Artie said, and he looked up, down, from side to

side. One could almost hear his mind clicking with excuses. "Oh," he said again.

"It would not, perchance, be due to the fact that you snuck out of the coal mine without me, would it?"

"Oh...well now. Hey!" He turned and faced forward. Again, the bunnies spun around. "Hey, I smell smoke!"

I looked over the side. A shudder ran through my frame. The lights of the first Siberian coal mine twinkled below, and in the distance stood an army of smokestacks belching out plumes of dense, black smoke. Even more disheartening, the bunnies once more came to rest over Artie's ears, but this time facing me.

They stared without blinking, their ruthless gazes fixed upon me, boring into me.

Soon the reindeer began to cough. Artie did too. Shreds of smoke drifted by like black phantoms; and then more, thicker and darker and rancid with fumes.

"We're almost there," Artie said. The bunnies continued to stare. A layer of coal dust had turned them from pure white to dull gray. Smoke settled into my lungs with every breath. "I'm going to set the sleigh down on the roof of the Blue Icicle," Artie said. "It's a little steep, but I think we'll manage."

A little steep. It was a peaked roof with a pitch so sharp that the only way to stay on top was for the reindeer to dangle from their harness on one side and the sleigh to hang on the other, like a larger version of Artie's earmuffs. We climbed in through a gable window and passed through dark hallways and down creaking stairways until we reached the main staircase. We crouched on the landing and gazed down upon a room filled with smoke, honky-tonk music, and snowmen. Carla, boisterous, buxom, and by far the heftiest snowmaid I had ever seen (but for her thin twig arms, as Artie had voiced, and rather comely icicle nose) served frozen drinks and bowls of sleet to the customers at the bar, all the while bellowing over the noise. "Hey Lulu!" she yelled to the snowmaid at the piano, "You got a request for 'Smoke Gets in Your Ice,'" and to a small snowboy with a woolen hat and two bottle caps for eyes she said, "Go down cellar, Perry, and bring up some more swizzle sticks."

"There!" Artie said, and pointed. "Look over there."

I craned my neck and squinted through the smoke. There stood the scoundrel himself, Frostwin, bent over a pool table with a thick cigar dangling from his lips and using his broomstick as a pool cue. "All right lads," he boomed to the other snowmen. "Place your bets!" A few of the snowmen set down poker chips on a side

table (one, I noticed, cheated by pulling off one of his eyes and adding it to his stack).

"That's him all right," I whispered to Artie. Thankfully he had left the earmuffs back in the sleigh so he had no trouble hearing me. "How can we convince him to come with us."

Artie thought for a moment. "Hmmm…"

Frostwin sent a snowball into a side pocket. The snowmen groaned. The one who cheated yelled, "I won, I won!"

Artie snapped his fingers. "You know that old silk hat he wears? The one he found?"

I nodded. "The one they say there must have been some magic in?"

"Yes. Look. It's down there on the bar. If we take it, he'll chase us. Happens every time. He loves that hat. It makes him dance around, or so I've heard."

"You can't trust those songs," I whispered. "Still…I've seen how he keeps a close eye on that hat, so it's worth a try. Sometimes Artie – not often – but sometimes, your ideas don't turn out half bad."

I could recount all the shenanigans that took place in the Blue Icicle. I could tell you how Carla threw her arms around Artie with a cry of, "Oh, my little honey elf, where have you *been?*" and nearly suffocated him. I could expound upon Lulu accusing me of spilling a hot toddy on her piano, which melted three of the black keys, and how three ruffians with ice picks for noses cornered me and demanded an explanation, and how – when I couldn't come up with one – they threw me straight over the bar and onto a moose head. I could tell you how Artie stole Frostwin's old silk hat, put it on his own head, and much to the surprise of all, began to laugh and dance around.

"There's no time for that!" I cried from the moose head.

"I can't help it!" Artie called. He twirled and pirouetted

and leaped and clicked his heels, all with an expression of demented horror upon his face, even as he laughed. "Oh my!" he yelled. "I can't stop! Ho-ho...hee-*heeee*! There must be – *hee-hee-heeeee* – there must have been some magic in this old silk hat I found!"

"Take it off!" I cried, which, to my mind, seemed an obvious solution, but before I could utter another word, Frostwin himself barged through the gathered patrons. "My hat!" he shouted. "Give it here! I found it first!"

He swung his broomstick. Artie ducked. The stick hit the hat and sent it in a line drive straight to the top of the moose head where it hit me square in the face, and though it didn't hurt, the jolt and the sheer surprise of it all sent me tumbling over the side. I threw the hat as I fell. Artie, racing up the stairs, caught it, and Frostwin barreled up after him, swinging his stick and cursing up a storm. (I could tell you all that he said, but I shall not for fear an Albanian orphan might read this. The disillusionment might prove fatal.)

Instead I shall inform you that we got Frostwin struggling and protesting into the sleigh, and somehow managed to get off the roof of the Blue Icicle and back into the air, and oh! What a wrenching, miserable ride lay before us. Frostwin had imbibed untold tumblers of rum punch (it seems unlikely we would have gotten him into the sleigh had it been otherwise). And loud? He hollered and hooted and waved to snowmen friends he *thought* were there, but weren't, and, worst of all, he bellowed the *same* part of the *same* song over and over again. "Sleigh bells ring! Are you listening? In the lane...no – Sleigh bells ring, are you listening? And...something glistening, and...No, wait. Sleigh bells ring. Are you listening?"

"Yes, I'm listening," I said.

"A beautiful sight, we're happy – no. Yes. No. What's the next part? Oh right. Sleigh bells ring! Are you glistening?"

I sighed. "Just stab me with an icicle. Please."

"In the lane, snow is listening!"

"Someone. Anyone. Just kill me."

I don't know if Artie heard me and took me at my word, but within moments, something happened that nearly fulfilled my request.

This is how Artie later likes to describe it. "You know how you're walking down an ice tunnel, and another elf is walking toward you, and you both see each other, and you both zig and zag, and swerve right and left, and somehow you *still* run into each other? Well, it was exactly like that." At which point I usually say, "No, it wasn't like that at all. We weren't in a tunnel, for one thing. We were in wide-open sky. And for another, that wasn't an elf walking toward us. It was a solid, brick smokestack over two hundred feet high. And – not to put too fine a point to it, but it wasn't walking at all. Not a step. It neither zigged nor zagged. It swerved neither left nor right. It stood there, the same as it had since the day it was made. And we – us – Artie and I – *we* also did not swerve, zig, nor zag. We ran straight into it."

"Not quite *into* it," Artie likes to point out, and in this I must admit he is not mistaken.

What happened was this: we took to the air, yes, but we also managed to fly through every cloud of smoke belching

from every smokestack. The cinders blinded those reindeer not already long-used to a sightless existence. Artie, too, could barely see. His face was smudged with black. His bunnies looked like fluffy crows. Even Frostwin broke off his infernal singing to cough and hack. We emerged from a particularly fog-like billow and there, right *there* before us stood the tallest smokestack of all, with something in Russian written down the side – "Watch Out," perhaps, or "Swerve if Thou Canst."

I gasped and cried, "Turn, Artie! Turn!"

"Up!" he yelled. "Gonner, up! *Up!*"

"What?" called the reindeer.

"Up! There's a…oh, *hee-hee*…straight ahead, a *ho-ho-ho*, a big something…"

And from the back: "Sleigh bells ring – are you listening?"

"Up, Gonner, up!"

The reindeer *finally* saw the solid wall of bricks directly in their path and swerved into a sharp, scimitar-like upward curve. The deer managed to avoid a collision – barely. We raced up the side, their hooves clacked on the top of the stack, and they flew into the billowing smoke. The sleigh followed and almost made it. The left runner slammed into an absurdly decorative capstone and snapped off in the front. We broke free of the smokestack but the runner, still attached in the rear, swung down under the sleigh and then up around the back where, with a mighty crack, it clobbered Frostwin on the back of the head, right in the middle of his three hundred and forty-sixth attempt at "Winter Wonderland."

You might have supposed that such a blow would have shattered his head into a million tiny snowflakes, each one a unique individual; but snowmen are made of tougher stuff than that. Instead, it acted upon him like Santa's slap on my back, the one that sent my front tooth flying to the window.

This is what I heard, exactly as I heard it:

"Sleigh bells ring, are you – *crack!*" Several small objects whizzed by my head, and then: "My eyes! My eyes! I can't see!"

I turned and gazed upon a completely blank face. The force of the blow had sent Frostwin's coal eyes and carrot nose flying from his head. "I can't see!" he cried. "I can't sniff!"

"Calm yourself!" I cried, rather un-calmly. "Calm yourself, I say! They're in here somewhere. They *must* be. Perhaps they – " I froze, rigid with horror at the sight of Artie's earmuffs eating Frostwin's nose. "Give me that," I said, but when I reached for the carrot the bunnies exposed their cruel, chisel-like teeth and snarled. Snarled!

I scrambled to the front seat. "Your earmuffs are eating his nose," I whispered to Artie. "His eyes are gone too!"

Frostwin clarified this last statement when he stood and began to feel his way around the sleigh, pawing both of us, and sobbing, "Oh the sky, the stars, I shall never see the moon again. I shall never sniff, nor snuffle, nor shall I evermore see nor smell the snow that glistens, nor the sleigh bells that listen. Never! Nevermore!"

On and on he went, and yes, it was a misfortune, a

tragedy even, but that did not alter the fact that I wanted – at that moment, and more than anything – to hurl him from the sleigh.

"Hey, I know!" Artie said, and with a few pulls on the reins and assorted shouts and commands, he guided the sleigh down behind one of the factories and landed right on top of the largest pile of coal I had ever seen. "This should work!" he said, and, reaching over the side, he picked up two pieces and plunked them onto Frostwin's face.

The snowman blinked once, then twice. "I can see!" he said, and raised his arms to the heavens. "I can *seeeeee*!" He lowered his gaze to the monstrous pile of coal beneath the sleigh, and in a voice of wonderment, exclaimed, "Well, what do you know! Just *look* at all the eyes!"

The snow bunnies had consumed Frostwin's nose long before we had a chance of saving it, and this upset him a great deal. Unlike the coal, we knew our chances of finding a pile of carrots in wintery Northern Siberia were slim at best, but Artie assured him we would procure for him a candy cane or similar appendage the moment we arrived back at the Pole.

We took to the air again, but before we had even touched the lowest clouds, we once more began to descend.

"What's happening?" I asked.

"I can't bear it," Artie said. "All this soot, these ashes. Look. The reindeer look like charcoal. My bunnies too. Even Frostwin. We can't return like this." We descended toward a grimy, low, one-story building with a brightly lit sign written in Russian – which Artie translated as "Ivan's Super Wash".

"I didn't know you could read Russian," I said, quite impressed.

"I can't. Well, I can order from a menu…you know, 'I'll have the cabbage,' and so forth. And I know a little about sleigh washes, but only because it's a particular hobby of mine. But that's really the extent of my Russian." He brought the sleigh to a surprisingly smooth landing in front of Ivan's Super Wash. "Just like at home!" he said, and rubbed his hands together. "And after we wash the sleigh, we'll be good as new."

The darkness inside made the reindeer nervous, but Artie urged them forward. They moved into the building. Their hooves clacked on the concrete floor. A door at the opposite end stood open, just like the washing barn back home. "A little more," Artie said. The reindeer pulled the sleigh inside, and there we sat. Nothing happened.

"Where are the elf washers?" I asked.

We waited. A reindeer shook his bells. Artie sniffed. Silence.

And then, softly… "Sleigh bells ring, are you – "

"Stop!" I cried. "Right now. Just *stop!*"

Silence. We waited.

Artie leaned toward a red button on the wall. "What's this for? You think it alerts the washers?"

"Could be," I said. "But maybe we shouldn't…"

Too late. He pressed it. Something began to hum, and then to shudder. It grew louder, and suddenly, out of nowhere, came jets of hot water, spewing over us from all sides. Some sort of waxy stuff mixed with multi-colored detergents spattered over us from above. The reindeer leaped and jangled in terror. "What happened?" Artie asked, and then – oh, how can I describe it?

Something whirred, an engine whined, and suddenly the most horrifying things – monstrous black brushes – came spinning down from the ceiling followed by ghastly arms of thick fabric, sloshing and grasping like soapy tentacles. The reindeer disappeared. "Oh hey!" I heard Gonner yell. "What's this? What's this?"

"Stop! Stop!" Artie yelled at the advancing brushes, as if hoping they might respond favorably; but it was but too late. "Hee-hee! Ha-*ho-ho!*" he shrieked as the brushes and serpentine tentacles flapped and slapped; the bunnies got tangled up and they too were spinning and slapping him. "Hee-hee-*heeeee!*" he screamed as the swirling, sudsy horror sucked him inside. "It's the end of the world!"

And then my turn. I tried to climb out the back, but one of the hideous brushes pulled me into the maelstrom where I was banged, bounced, squirted, scrubbed, soaked, whirled, and then nearly blown from the sleigh by jets of hot air whistling over us like a storm off the Sahara. We emerged from the house of horror shaken and terrified, but clean as a whistle. The reindeer were bright and fluffy. Their bells and harness buckles sparkled like silver. Artie was the cleanest I had ever seen him. His bunnies were as white as newly fallen snow, and the sleigh glistened and sparkled for the first time in several hundred years. I, too, felt like a new Elf, all scrubbed and shiny, and I was about to remark upon my newfound sense of well-being when, "Look!" Artie cried with a gasp of horror.

I turned in the seat and found myself sitting beside…I didn't know what. A thing. A thin, translucent, shining something.

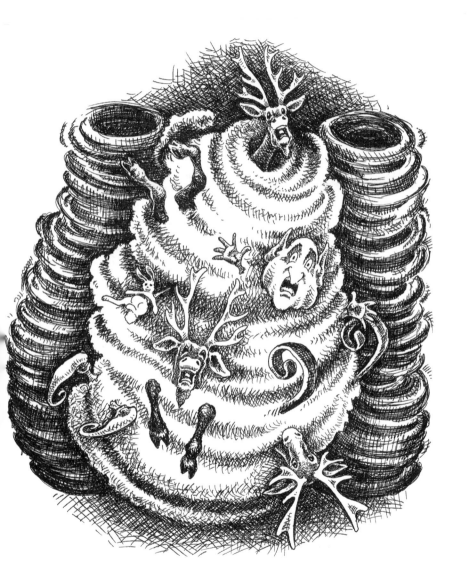

"Sleigh bells ring," it sang in a squeezed, muffled voice. "Are you listening?"

Frostwin! Whereas a vicious crack on the head by a sleigh runner may have little untoward effect upon a snowman, it appears the same cannot be said for a bath in boiling water. He melted down into the thinnest, clearest, most appalling icicle I have ever seen, with two cleanly shimmering pieces of coal stuck to it, one on each side.

And that was the sight we presented, when Santa opened the door and yelled, "And here you are, children! I promised to bring him to you, and I have. Behold! Frosty the Snow-" Shrieks of terror drowned him out as a hundred or so Albanian orphans gazed upon Frostwin the Icicle-man for the first time. Things were made infinitely worse by the fact that Artie, only moments before, had persuaded Frostwin to try on a new nose. A carrot? No. A plunger retrieved from the reindeer barn, with the handle end jammed into the ice between the coal eyes, and the round rubber head jutting out like a gaping mouth at the end of a hideously long and narrow snout. Santa stared, his mouth agape. The Albanians shrieked and cried. Artie, alas, chose that very moment to put the old silk hat on Frostwin's pointed head, which made him start to laugh and dance around in the most ghastly manner possible.

I could tell you how the orphans, mad with terror,

began to dash about in confused, screeching circles, and how Frostwin, rather insulted by this, began to chase them and swing at them with his broomstick, and how he only paused a moment when he heard Santa holler "Stop!", which alarmed his bodyguards and once again persuaded them to pile onto me and pinion my arms behind my head. And I could tell you how Santa demanded an explanation from us and how we couldn't come up with one, and how he forgot what he had demanded when we *did* come up with one, and completely misunderstood our explanation and somehow thought we were asking to be transferred back to the coalmines for another season.

I could tell you all that, but I shall not.

I shall save that for another day.

Juniper Dodd
And The Rein-critters

The great North Woods is full of interesting things. Trees, for example. We have lots of trees. We have lots of moose, too, especially in those mucky places beside the road up past Colebrook. We have black bear, and white-tailed deer, and wild turkeys; and we have people from around Boston coming up with their snow machines every winter, and in summer too, up visiting the Flume or to look up at the place where the Old Man of the Mountain used to gaze down upon them with stony eyes. He slipped off the mountain during an ice storm several years ago and now he's just a flat, empty cliff – which might well end up as New Hampshire's new state symbol since I don't know what else we could put on our signs.

Another thing we have no shortage of is cantankerous, crusty old men, the kind you see on TV every four years when primary season rolls around, walking in the snow in front of a dairy barn while a tanned newscaster with dazzling teeth describes them, inevitably, as "contrarian".

The Christmas Mink

I know two of those old contrarians fairly well, Juniper Dodd and Maurice Turquotte, both approaching seventy, and both as cantankerous and crusty as they come. They're close with their money too, especially Maurice. Tight-fisted, crabby, and far edgier and more disagreeable than Juniper, Maurice is about the last person you might associate with Christmas. Oh, he's lived through many holiday seasons, and maybe even enjoyed one or two of them, but he's hardly a paragon of good cheer (neither is Juniper for that matter, though he at least cracks a smile now and then); yet the two old rascals *are* inescapably associated with Christmas by most in our town.

Why? Because every year, just after Thanksgiving, they spend day after day in the woods gathering spruce boughs, and nearly every evening in December they sit inside Juniper's barn making wreaths. It's a nice place to visit, almost as nice as Tiny and Madge's donkey barn. I go to Juniper's quite often. They don't talk much, and I like the cool, clean smell of the winter barn: the hay, the smoke from Juniper's pipe, and mostly the spicy wintery fragrance of the spruce boughs. Juniper has a woodstove he keeps roaring most hours. On the coldest days, I've seen the stovepipe turn cherry-red, that's how hot it gets. And there's always a kettle left on a slow boil for tea.

Wreathing isn't the most lucrative enterprise but it gives the two old coots something to do – that's the main reason

158

they go to all the trouble, I think. Last year Maurice's share came to $181.50. Now you would think someone like Maurice would squirrel it away as soon as he could, and most of the time that's exactly what he does. He squirrels every cent away, either in the First Cranberry Bank or (some say) in a hollow log down by the blueberry bog. Last year was different. He made $181.50 in wreath sales, but by Christmas morning, all but fifty cents of it was gone.

This is how it went:

Some of you might remember Billy O'Keefe, who used to work over at the lumberyard. He lived near Juniper's house, up past where the old icehouse used to be before it burned. You might not remember Billy, but maybe you recall the car accident last year, the one near the railroad trestle. You can still see the gash in that big pine tree…anyway, two guys died in that crash, and one of them was Billy O'Keefe. The other was a guy from Maine…something Duntley. Can't remember his first name.

Anyway. Billy, of course, didn't have any insurance, and his wife Kate and their five or six kids…let me think. Jimmy, Tom, Mary-Margaret, Ryan… who else? Meghan. So that makes five. No, six. I forgot Sally. Six kids. So Billy left Kate and their six kids without much at all. They didn't have too much when he was alive either, so it wasn't all that long a slide to where they ended

159

up, which was pretty much with nothing. Kate must have had some kind of Social Security, and I know there was a program in town that provided a turkey for Thanksgiving, so they weren't completely penniless or hungry. Still, I don't know how big the turkeys were, or if they were any good, so things couldn't have been easy for them.

I ran into Kate at Cumberland Farms a week or two before Christmas and I asked her how things were going. She said they were making due, but it was little sad for them (the first year without Billy, of course). It was made especially sad because she felt she had to talk to the kids about "you know who."

Well, no, I didn't know who.

"Santa," said one of the little ones, probably Sally. "Mama says he won't be able to come to our house this year. He's going to come next year. Right, Mama?"

Kate smiled, "That's right, sugar." Her smile faded as she looked at me and shrugged her shoulders, as if to say, "What else could I tell them?"

"Well, that's awful tragic, ain't it?" Juniper said when I told him. Maurice grunted and reached for another spruce bough. They said little else while I was there and I didn't bring up the subject again. Instead, we talked about…I don't remember now what we talked about, guess it wasn't important. I left soon after, and Juniper and Maurice sat beside the stove without saying a word, working on their wreaths, attaching spruce greens to the wire hoop or tying red ribbons. The livestock watched from the stalls with mild interest.

Juniper has quite a collection of farm animals. He calls them his "critters". He has a big workhorse named Warren and a little Jersey cow named Mo (short for Maureen). He has two goats called Brownie and Daisy and a sheep named Edith. His barn cat is a tabby named Alice, and… who else? Oh yeah, Tippy. Can't forget him, Juniper's big old hound dog.

So there they were, Juniper and Maurice and all the critters in the barn, when right out of the blue Juniper asked Maurice how much wreath money they had, and Maurice said: "Three hundred and sixty-three, so far… which comes to one hundred eighty one and fifty cents each." (Maurice, himself, told me all about this later, in case you're wondering how I know about it. Juniper lies a good deal, and I never believe a word he says, but Maurice you can sort-of trust.)

So Maurice told Juniper how much wreath money they had made. Juniper rubbed his chin, which nearly sent Maurice running from the barn. Juniper rubbing his chin over money often means that he's come up with a scheme to make more, which usually leaves everyone involved a good deal more poverty-stricken than when they started. I should know – I'm still out seventy-five bucks since his "Let's pour concrete into a plastic kiddy pool and draw Franklin Roosevelt's profile on it and sell them as wicked big dimes to people from Massachusetts" scheme. Unfortunately, none of us could draw Franklin Roosevelt, so we ended up with enormous concrete portraits of someone that resembled – not FDR – but one of those bird things that dip their beak in a glass of water and then pop up and swing back and forth for a while before they once again lower their beak in the fluid. These particular Rooseveltian "birds" suffer further indignities due to several unfortunate misspellings in the wording above their heads – "In God we Turst," for instance – and since we never figured out how to reuse the kiddie pools, we ended up ruining each one we bought. That, along with the concrete, set us each back about seventy-five dollars. And did we sell any? Not a one.

Juniper ended up using them as a retaining wall for his cucumber garden.

I was no longer in the barn when he started to rub his chin, for which I was and remain grateful. He rubbed his chin, and Maurice started to get all panicky, and when Juniper told him his newest scheme, Maurice clamped his arms over his chest, planted his feet firmly on the floor, and scowled. "Nope," he said. "Not gonna do it."

"I'm not asking for *all* of it," Juniper said. "Just a few bucks to do something good."

"I don't want to do something good. Every time you want to do something good it turns out as something bad."

"Oh, come on," said Juniper. "This time will be different."

"It won't be different, and I ain't doing it. And besides, no one will believe it."

"They will, Maurice. Trust me."

They went on like that, around and around until Juniper finally convinced Maurice to go along with his scheme. "But only if I don't have to pay for it. Promise me, June – not a single dime."

"My sacred word of honor," Juniper said, and laid his hand over his heart.

This was his scheme:

Years before, the two scoundrels had "borrowed" a big canvas laundry hamper from the hospital down in Colebrook. They had had a few too many one night and thought it might be a fun idea to remove it from the hospital grounds, a notion undoubtedly suggested by the lettering stenciled on its side: "Upper Connecticut Valley Hospital: Do Not Remove."

Juniper's idea was to nail an old pair of skis to the bottom of the laundry hamper. "And where are we going to get skis?" Maurice asked. Juniper reminded him that they had "borrowed" some about ten years before from the old ski lodge on Rascals Mountain. "Still have 'em up in the hay loft," he said, and continued to outline his plan. "We'll nail 'em to the bottom of the hamper...it makes a sort of sleigh, y'see? And then we'll attach a few reindeer to the front and off we'll go to the O'Keefe house, and by golly, we'll *prove* to them O'Keefe kids that Santa didn't pass them by, whether they like it or not."

"Well, it'll prove *something*," Maurice said. "And Juniper – now don't get mad. I'm not suggesting it's a dumb idea or anything...well, actually, yes, that's exactly what I'm suggesting. It's a dumb idea."

"Is not."

"Is."

"Is not."

"Is. And I can prove it with two words."

"Which are...?"

"*Rein*. That's one. And *deer*. That's two."

Juniper scrunched up his face and bit his lower lip.

"Aha!" crowed Maurice. "Reindeer! The ointment in the fly! You can look all you want, but you won't find hide nor hair of a reindeer, not hereabouts anyway. Whitetail, yes. Rein? No."

"Good point."

"No, it's a *great* point. Now let's drop the whole foolish idea – a laundry hamper sleigh? For heaven sake, let's just drop it and get back to wreathing."

They did. They made a wreath apiece, and had no sooner started in on a second when Juniper threw his wire frame and spruce bough to the floor and pointed toward the stalls. "There they are!" he cried.

Startled, Maurice spun about, not knowing what he might find. "There who are?" And then it dawned. "You mean them?" He gestured toward the stalls. "The critters? As *reindeer*?"

"Why not?"

"Because you can't have – well, just look at them! You can't have rein-goats and a rein-cow. No kid in his right mind will believe Santa is being hauled about by a rein-goat."

"We'll disguise them. Warren and Mo too. And Tippy, he'll make a fine reindeer." Tippy, the rein-hound, looked up at them with those sad eyes of his and wagged his tail in a languid, back-and-forth way, as if his tail knew what was coming and wanted no part of it, yet couldn't quite summon the energy to run away.

That Christmas Eve, Maurice and Juniper gathered some of their finest spruce boughs and stuck them onto belts with glue and string and tied them around the heads of the sheep, the dog, and Warren the horse. Things were easier with the goats and Mo the cow as they simply tied the boughs to their horns, and Lord, there has never been a more ridiculous spectacle than those poor mortified

animals with spruce boughs sticking up from their heads, looking nothing at all like antlers. Even the goats and cows who *had* antler-like appendages now looked like they had somehow lost them and tried, half-heartedly, to replace them with something that would in no way remind them of their loss.

Juniper looked only slightly less ridiculous. He didn't have a Santa suit so he wore a red hunting coat over his long red underdrawers and two big black rubber boots, out of which rose his skinny legs like those of a scarlet ibis. Instead of a Santa hat he wore his usual hunting cap with earflaps, but with a red ribbon pinned to the top in the forlorn hope of making it look like a stocking cap. He then donned a beard made with some wool "borrowed" from Edith the sheep.

Maurice wore green, a smaller woolen beard, and a knit cap with so many holly twigs jammed into it that, from the back, his head looked like an evergreen porcupine.

Only Alice the orange tabby, too small and far too dignified to take part, remained untouched by the foolishness. She perched on top of a barrel, licking her paws and gazing upon the scene with regal disdain while Maurice and Juniper attached a rope to the hamper and tried to figure out a way to harness up the rein critters. They put Warren in the lead as they assumed he would be best suited to plow through the snow. Everyone else lined up behind him, looking as embarrassed as they could possibly be – especially Tippy, who appeared positively miserable and wilted under Alice's scornful gaze. He tried to scratch his antlers off with his hind leg and Juniper said, "Oh come on Tip. Be a good sport."

The good sport whimpered and sulked.

Two days earlier, they had visited the Dollar Store where Juniper bought a cartload of dolls and toys and plastic cars and such. Maurice did not participate in this phase of the plan. "Remember, a promise is a promise," he said. "Not a single penny." After jamming the toys into an old Blue Seal grain bag, Maurice helped Juniper into the hamper, and then picked up a flashlight and a set of "borrowed" sleigh bells. Off they went into the woods where they got hung up on roots and bogged down in mire. The harness slipped twice and broke once, an antler snapped off a goat, and the belt holding Tippy's antlers slid down around his neck, with the antlers themselves hovering over his back like angel wings.

The rein-critters simply did not know what was expected of them. They tried to wander off in six different directions at once, and because it was so dark, poor Warren kept entangling himself in brambles or colliding into trees. The second or third time he did this, Mo, who was directly behind him, caught him in the haunches with her horns (her real ones), which sent Warren into the pines at a brisk trot, which hauled the rest of the rein-critters forward with a lurch, which then sent Juniper over the back of the hamper where he landed flat on his back in the snow.

"For the love'a Mike, Warren!" he hollered as he chased after the sleigh and, with Maurice's help, managed to haul his gangly frame back inside. "Watch what you're doing.

Land sakes, but that was a surprise." He sat down again beside the grain bag. Warren moved deeper into the pines, and then tried to back out of them again before scraping along the length of the trees. Boughs released their burdens of snow on the other rein-critters and the two in the sleigh. "This isn't working at all," Juniper said, brushing snow from his shoulders. "Maurice, why don't you get out there and take the lead with your flashlight."

"I'm not wearing no antlers," Maurice insisted as he climbed from the hamper.

"Don't have to," Juniper said, and added with a chuckle, "But Maurice with your nose so bright, won't you guide my sleigh tonight?"

"Nose so bright," Maurice sputtered as he moved to the head of the team. Warren seemed relieved to have some light shed on the subject, and equally relieved to give up his Rudolphian position. They moved through the woods at a faster pace then, and without so many interruptions caused by unexpected collisions or tangled harnesses, but once they came within sight of the O'Keefe house, the true ridiculous extent of the endeavor became horribly clear, at least to Maurice. "This isn't going to work," he fretted, and shined the flashlight in Juniper's eyes. "What the heck are we doing here anyway? No one is going to believe you're Santa – skinny as a rail, with them droopy underdrawers and an old hunting coat…it won't work!"

"How do you know?" Juniper asked, his voice muffled behind his sheep's wool beard.

"*Anyone* would know! Look at these things, these critters! No one in their right mind could possibly believe they're reindeer."

"Ho-ho-ho!" Juniper hollered so suddenly that the

startled livestock reared up and, in unison, bleated, whinnied, bellowed and barked with a collective sound not often heard outside a county fair.

"Oh shush," Maurice said, holding Warren by the halter. "Nothing to be ascared of."

Again - "Ho-ho-ho!" This time the animals looked back over their shoulders, as though wondering what on earth could have gotten into him. "Jingle those bells, Maurice."

"Do you have to be so loud?"

"I want them to know Santa's coming."

"Well, tone it down a bit. They're liable to think he's arriving on a circus train."

"On Dasher!" Juniper hollered, and Maurice winced. "On Prancer and Cupid and…what's the rest of them? On Donner and something-something. On everybody!" he boomed, and Maurice rang the bells as hard as he could while the rein-critters strained and pulled and dragged the hamper over the gravel driveway into the O'Keefe's dooryard.

A curtain moved behind a window and they heard a little squeal, soon joined by another and another, louder and louder, until they heard all kinds of screeching and hollering inside, followed by a clattering and bumping of running feet, and then the boom and squeak of the front door opening.

Kate O'Keefe stood in the doorway, hovering midway between a burst of laughter and a flood of tears, with her eyes wide and her hand held over her mouth to stifle either a sob or a smile (it was hard to tell which).

Her children gathered close around her. "You said he wouldn't come!" said one of the younger ones. Kate lowered her hand to respond, but couldn't; her hand came up to cover her mouth again.

"Ho-ho-ho, Katie O'Keefe" cried Juniper Claus in the lowest, deepest voice he could muster. "Can it be that our little plan actually worked? Is it true – is it *really* true that all the little O'Keefes thought I'd forgotten about them this year?"

"I..." was all Kate could say, but one of the older kids (who *surely* must have realized the truth) said, "It was a joke! Mama played a joke on us!" and like rabbits pouring out of a hole, the O'Keefe clan dashed into the yard, hollering and jumping up and down, and shouting out to Santa Claus. Some of them climbed into the sleigh with "Upper Connecticut Valley Hospital: Do Not Remove" written on the side; others patted the goats, the sheep, the cow, dog and horse, and said, "Look Mama – reindeers! You ever seen real reindeers before?"

They climbed all over Juniper and laughed and said they always, deep down, knew he was coming, and Juniper with his droopy red underwear and hunting coat laughed and ho-ho'd and opened the Blue Seal grain bag.

Sally, the youngest O'Keefe, tugged on Maurice's sleeve. "Are you an elf?"

Maurice stared straight ahead, cleared his throat, and rubbed his nose with the flashlight. "Yeah."

"Look Mama!" she cried. "An elf!"

Juniper handed out the presents, all of them wrapped in week-old sections of the *Colebrook News and Sentinel*, and every O'Keefe kid screeched when they opened them. "Look! It's just what I wanted! Look Mama – he heard me. He read my letter!" After everything was given out, Ryan O'Keefe, the youngest of the boys, stood on tiptoe and peered over the edge of the hamper. "Santa?"

Juniper spun around, startled by the tiny sound. "Yes, my lad?"

"What about Mama?"

Juniper stared at Maurice, eyes wide, mouth hanging open. "Oh my Lord," he whispered, and then turned back to little Ryan. "Oh, I guess…"

A long, awkward pause. Very awkward. Warren pawed the ground. Juniper scratched his chin under his beard. The pause lengthened into deeper realms of awkwardness until - "Santa…" said Maurice.

"Yes, elf?"

"I just remembered…" Maurice bore a pained expression, as if heartburn or a sudden migraine had flared up. "Back at the North Pole, you told me…" He hesitated.

"What did I tell you?"

"Ummm…you told me…"

"Come, come, elf. Spit it out."

"You-told-me-to-hold-this-for-Katie-O'Keefe,"
Maurice said with a sudden rush of words, as if hoping
to get through an unpleasant ordeal as quickly as possible,
the way one does when walking across hot coals or taking
cod liver oil. He closed his eyes and grimaced, and with the
greatest reluctance possible, reached into his pocket and
pulled out a wad of cash, folded, rolled, and bound with
several thick elastic bands – his wreath money, one hundred
and eighty-one dollars, though he kept the additional fifty
cents (one quarter, two dimes and nickel) hidden in his
front pocket. Like a condemned criminal he handed the
roll of bills to Sally. "For your Ma," he
said, looking as if he might cry.

Kate took the money from
Sally and handed it back to him.
"No," she whispered, "you've
done enough."

Maurice grinned and nodded and
started to put the money back into his
pocket, but Juniper stopped him. "Elf!" he shouted. "Give
it back! That's to pay for heating oil."

Maurice closed his eyes again and handed it over with
another grimace. Kate grabbed him around the shoulders
and planted a kiss on his cheek, then leaned into the sleigh
and did the same to Juniper. "I'll never forget this," she
said, and pulling her sweater tight against her neck, she
walked back to the house. "Come on, kids. It's cold out
here. Santa has a lot of places to visit," and standing in the
doorway, surrounded by her children, she waved good-bye,
and all the little O'Keefes waved and called good-bye as
the rein-critters began to move.

"Merry Christmas!" Juniper yelled. "Merry Christmas

to all, and to all a good night! And...and he rode out of sight, while someone pulled up the sash! Ma in her kerchief, I think it was. Merry Christmas!"

"Merry Christmas," Maurice muttered so low that no one but Warren could have heard him.

The sleigh jolted, Juniper called out, and Maurice rang his bells as the rein critters pulled away from the house and they once again entered the dark of the woods.

"Well, Maurice "Elf" Turquotte, I never thought I'd live to see the day!"

"It's your fault," Maurice sputtered. "If you hadn't roped me into this foolish enterprise, it would never have happened. And don't you dare tell anyone I gave away all that money – what was I thinking, what in the world came over me? And *especially* don't you dare tell anyone I was an elf. I wasn't an elf."

"Were."

"Wasn't. Wasn't then, ain't now. I'm not an elf, never was. Never made a toy in my life."

"The kids believed you were."

"Well, so what? They believed a nut in a laundry hamper was Santa Claus."

Juniper chuckled and lit his pipe and laid back in the hamper with one booted skinny leg draped over the other, and they made their way through the quiet woods. The bells jingled. Warren snorted. "Strange, isn't it?" Juniper asked without taking his pipe from between his teeth.

"What is?"

"Think about it. How could those kids believe we were really Santa and his reindeer?"

"And an elf," Maurice added.

"Right!" Juniper said, and took his pipe from his mouth and used it to punctuate the air. "Can't forget the elf! But really...how *could* they believe it?"

"Who knows?" Maurice said. "Maybe they wanted to, that's all."

"Maybe."

They arrived back at the barn and took off their beards and unharnessed the rein-critters. Juniper gave them all an extra portion of grain (all but Tippy who was perfectly happy to get a stale cupcake). Maurice poked around inside the stove until the coals brightened, and they both looked around the barn.

Christmas Eve. Wreath season had come to an end. Spruce boughs and needles littered the floor. Odds and ends of ribbons hung from the stalls.

Juniper relit his pipe. Maurice sat on a bale of hay. He reached into his front pocket and pulled out the quarter, two dimes and a nickel and jingled them in his hand before putting them into his pocket again. "Juniper?"

"Yup?"

"Maybe we ought'a clear away these boughs."

"Good idea."

Maurice grabbed a broom and started to sweep the needles.

Juniper reached for a ribbon. "Wasn't a bad wreath season on the whole, was it?"

"Nope. Not bad at all." Maurice opened the door and pushed the broom. Spruce needles spread from the doorway in the shape of a fan. "Oh, look at that."

"What?" Juniper asked, and joined him at the door.

"It's snowing."

"Well, what do you know," he whispered. Their shadows

The Christmas Mink

fell over the spruce needles, and over their shadows the snow fell, soft and light. They watched it for a long time. Warren snorted in his stall. Fire crackled in the stove. Behind them, Tippy yawned and scratched his ear.

A Timberman's Tree

When I was a boy, there was an old house up on
the ridge, just before the Twombley cemetery.
You can still see the road that leads to it, though it doesn't
really look like a road, only two tracks side-by-side heading
up into the woods. A man lived there, crazy as a loon,
named Tim. I don't remember his last name – O'Donnell,
O'Connor, O'something or other, but that doesn't matter
because no one called him anything but Timberman.
He was older than I am now when I knew him, but my
grandfather knew him when he was a kid. They were about
the same age, which would make them about a hundred
and forty years old if they were still around today.

Tim was always a little strange, or so my grandfather
said. I can hear him now, sitting by that old Franklin stove
in the garage, saying, "Yup, that Tim...always a little
strange. Even when he was a young lad. Didn't play with
no one, hardly ever spoke to no one, kept to his-self mostly,
wandering in the woods at all times and in all weathers

– night, winter, summer, day, rain, snow, sun; it didn't matter. I heard more than one deer hunter say they'd run into him high up on the ridge, all on his own, wandering…"

One day when Tim was about maybe eight or nine, he was on one of his lonesome wanderings when he came across a small spindly tree in a clearing, a hemlock spruce with three sickly branches and a trunk not half so big around as my thumb. It wasn't shaped funny. It wasn't red or purple or any other unusual color. Nothing special, nothing unusual; even its spindly weakness didn't set it apart as there were plenty of others exactly like it in the clearing.

But something happened to Tim when he saw it.

He fell in love with it.

Imagine that - someone falling in love with a tree! It wasn't romantic love, of course, but a different kind, more like the love I feel for my dog Tucker, or Aunt Mary does for her cats, or any one of us feel toward our best friend – our *very* best friend. Tim started going up there every day, summer and winter, rain or sun, sometimes skipping school so he could go up on the mountainside to sit beside the little tree.

Someone followed him one day to see what he was up to and where he went all the time, and he came back to town and said that Tim had been up in the woods, visiting a tree, which sounded more than a little ridiculous. "Why, he just happened to sit down beside it to rest," someone

said, and another said, "Of course, that must be the case."
The first someone followed Tim again the next day, and
the day after that, and brought a few of the other someones
along so they could see for themselves; and it soon became
clear that the first someone had spoken true. Tim was
visiting a tree.

The town was different back then. There's a lot of talk
about the past and the good old days, but most of it is based
in rose-colored memories unaffected by fact. Oh sure, this
town truly *was* different back in those days, but not in a rose-
colored way, that's for sure. It bordered on outright warfare.
Something had gone wrong somewhere…I believe it may
have started with an
argument involving
a '37 Chevy, though
I can't be certain.
Something happened –
we know that much
– and it caused an
enormous amount
of bickering and
squabbling, and
even the occasional
knock-down, drag-out fistfight. The Reillys did not like
the McGlaughlins, the O'Briens fought openly with the
Letourneaus, and old man Henderson wouldn't give the
time of day to old man Anderson.

Nobody, absolutely nobody, could have told you what
the fight was about or why the town was so divided. The
'37 Chevy's role in this had long since faded from memory,
but the bitterness and ill will remained and took on a life of

its own. And you can well imagine what a town filled with feuding, backbiting, miserable gossip-mongers thought when they heard about Tim and his tree. Each side eagerly delegated him to the other; front porches hissed with whispers of "Oh, he's related to so-and-so"; and in the Spruce bar, one could hear "That sort of thing runs in their blood" over shots of whisky.

Tim's parents hoped to put a stop to it. Like most parents, they had an aversion to gossip about their children, especially when it involved an evergreen. "A tree!" his father cried. "I could understand a bicycle or a dog…but Tim, a tree? Nobody in his right mind has a tree for a best friend!"

Alas, Tim's father had it right - not about the tree, but about his son's state of mind. I might as well say it right now: Tim was different. He *wasn't* in his right mind. Oh, yes, some threw around cruel words like "slow" to describe him, but most eventually settled on "dim", which had an attractive poetic quality the others lacked.

Dim Tim.

The situation grew worse as he grew older. Other boys went to dances and started dating, but not Tim. His mother, no doubt hoping for grandchildren rather than seedlings, cried in despair. His distraught father tried to talk some sense into him. "This is how it is," he said. "You're a man now. And that is a tree. I don't care how much you like it, it's still a tree. That's all it will ever be – a tree."

Tim seemed perfectly fine with that.

Around this time, a joke began to make the rounds. Someone saw him in the woods and asked, "Hey Dim Tim, when you gonna cut down that tree?" and Tim smiled a bashful smirky little smile and said, "Not yet."

It wasn't really a joke – quite obviously, when you consider the lack of humor involved – but it took hold and became a greeting of sorts. Instead of "hello, how are you?" everyone asked when he was going to cut the tree down, and Tim, instead of returning a "fine, thank you," only smiled shyly and said, "Not yet."

By the time he turned eighteen, the tree had grown much taller than he could ever hope to be, but it remained as typical and uninteresting a spruce as you could ever hope to find. Its boughs had filled out, it sprouted some new branches, and its trunk had grown stronger, but no more so than its neighbors. None of that mattered to Tim. He continued to visit it every day and spent hours circling it on foot, looking at each needle on every bough, as though memorizing them for his dreams. Sometimes, in the summer, he took a blanket to the mountain and slept beneath it, close to its trunk, and he woke in the morning to see it tall above him, grey and glistening with dew in the early morning glow, as perfect in his waking sight as it had been in his sleeping mind.

Tim left home eventually and took a job as a lumberjack with the Butler Timber Company. I know, I know – it surprised everyone. A lumberjack! No one would have guessed that someone with his peculiar obsession would apply for such a job, or that he would be so good at it. It surprised his father too. "Well!" he said, clapping his hands together with pleasure. "A lumberjack, eh? You wouldn't happen to want to start with a certain you-know-what that's been a thorn in this family's side for years, would you?"

"No," said Dim Tim (now known as Tim the Dim Timberman), no, he would not.

"Not yet."

He was still tree-mad, but qualified his ailment by proving he was only mad about that one, single, solitary tree.

All others fell before his axe. He swung and chopped and cut and felled, and soon rose in rank and, in the eyes of his co-workers became the most skilled lumberjack working the timber fields. His way with an axe impressed them, and they admired him for it, but they knew about the spruce and were a little wary. He never socialized with the other lumberjacks; he never drank; he never smoked; he never brought women into the camp; he never did anything but save his money and visit his old friend on the mountain whenever he had a little free time.

Eventually he saved enough money to buy the land surrounding the tree and, of course, the tree itself. He built a little house covered with tar-paper and roofed with cast-off slabs from the lumber mill. Then he cleared away all the other spruce, maple and oak on his property, which served to make his special one appear bigger, taller and fuller than it really was; and still, whenever someone in town asked when was going to cut it down, he said, "Not yet."

By the time I arrived on the scene, my grandfather, the Timberman and that tree of his were all getting old. With sun and lots of clear space and mountain air, the spruce grew to an enormous height and reigned like a green emperor, with Tim's small tarpaper shack huddling like a groveling peasant beneath its regal boughs.

Tim never lost interest in his friend. Indeed, the higher it grew and the more lush and expansive became its boughs, the more the Timberman revered it.

You'd think after over sixty years a person might grow weary of giving so much time and energy and…well, *love*, toward something that never gave a thing in return. It couldn't talk to him. It couldn't reach out on its own to touch him. It could do little beyond providing a patch of shade in the summer and a bit of protection from the winter wind - both nice things, but a little paltry when one considers the investment.

I remember Tim the Dim Timberman walking the streets of town. He seemed older than time, all crooked and bent as he walked, with his hair as white as mine is now, but he still had strong arms from all his years of swinging an axe, and his face was always bright and glowing. I remember asking him, "Hey Timberman, when you gonna cut down that tree?" – the same as I had heard everyone else ask whenever he passed. I was a little boy then, and I laughed when I said it. Terrible, isn't it, to laugh at an older person like that, even if he was a little crazy? But the Timberman never got mad. He smiled at me, the same as he did to all the others, and said in that cracked, gravelly voice of his, "Not yet."

One Christmas Eve, we heard a knock at the door followed by a rush of wind as one of our neighbors stormed in to tell us the mountain was on fire. Those were his words: "The mountain is on fire!" I imagined a conflagration roaring from the lake at its base all the way to its summit – a true spectacle if ever there was one – but when we went outside to look, I saw only a disappointing glow above the far treetops. It might have been impressive and even a bit alarming had our neighbor not been so extravagant in his warning, but even so, I was surprised it caused so much commotion. Snow covered the ground so no one feared it might spread, but then the church bell started to peal out the steady clanging call for the Volunteer Fire Department and we knew it was a house fire.

Our hearts sank. We were embroiled in the same endless, pointless feuds as everyone else in town, but still, the idea of someone's – anyone's – house going up in flames on Christmas Eve was a dreadful thought. My father and grandfather, my uncles and cousins and I threw on our coats and boots and headed for the church where the volunteers gathered to await instructions. They stamped their feet against the cold and those that smoked clenched their cigarettes and pipes between their teeth to prevent them from chattering.

"Whose house is it?" they asked, but no one seemed to know.

Someone – Juniper Dodd claims it was his father, but he fibs a good deal so no one believes him – but someone came out of the church and told the men to go home and get their wives and children and head up to the Timberman's shack on the ridge.

"Is it on fire?" they asked, knowing full well a frail little shack like that would have collapsed in ashes by the time they reached it.

"Just go get your families," he insisted.

Some grumbled over this, and a couple of arguments broke out – but what else is new? We did that over much less than a fire on Christmas Eve.

"All right, everyone, get ready," my father said as he came through the door stomping the snow off his boots. "Bundle up, it's cold out there."

"Where are we going?" my mother asked, and she peered through the window, alarmed by the possibility that a spark had somehow, miraculously, descended over hill and dale, snow and ice, to land intact and flaming on our side porch.

"I don't know," my father said in a voice both weary and agitated. "We're going to see the fire, I guess."

"But we have so much to do!" my mother protested. "I have a pie in the oven. And it's cold out there!"

She wasn't the only one. Tempers flared on the road

that night. Families squabbled amongst themselves, or shouted out insults to those they passed. No one knew why we were drawn to the fire, especially those unrelated to members of the Fire Department, but something in the man's voice – the man at the church – compelled us all out into the snow, abandoning the warmth of our houses and our turkeys, hams and pies in our ovens.

We saw the fire through the pines long before we arrived. Clouds shuddered with gold and orange light from below, and when we turned into the clearing and drove onto the Timberman's property, the cars slowed and stopped, and we all got out to stare in wonder, dazed and silent but for the crunch of snow beneath our boots as we shuffled closer, closer, closer to the tree.

Sparkling, shimmering lights, thousands of them in every color and every shade of every imaginable color twinkled from every bough, even the highest. Golden balls and silver bells, spangles and beads and tinsel hung in such profusion they nearly hid the green beneath, and when the wind rose and the tree swayed, a riot of tiny bells jingled with a sound like a thousand horse-drawn sleighs. High at the top, high above everything else, burned a golden star, and beyond that hung a billion more, seemingly there to watch over the tree, envious of its light and studying its brilliance in hopes that, one day, they too might shine as bright.

We gathered around the foot of the great Christmas tree like warmly dressed presents, all of us as open-mouthed and wide-eyed as could be. I, for one, had never seen anything so beautiful before.

No one remembers how it happened, but most think it began when someone arrived in a pick-up truck loaded

with jugs of hot apple cider. Soon bottles of rum and brandy were opened, and before long everyone was either cidering or brandying before one of the small fires we had built in the clearing. And then someone started to hum a Christmas carol, and before long, all the little fireside clusters began to sing.

People who hadn't shared a civil word in twenty years now toasted each other's health and happiness. The O'Briens and Letourneaus shared a fire, and when Mr. McGlaughlin brought out his penny whistle, the men in each family danced with women from another. I chased children I was forbidden to play with across the snow, and they chased me back to the fires, while old man Henderson and old man Anderson linked arms and sang the decidedly non-seasonal "Beautiful Isle of Capri" until they lost their voices.

"Where's the Timberman?" someone finally asked, and that's when we began to notice what we should have seen at once. "Hey, that's right," said another. "He must have done this. Where is he?"

We looked around the clearing, and knocked on his door, but saw no sign of the eccentric old man. Someone called to him – "Tim!" – and then we all did, calling in one, loud, boisterous voice: "Tim! Dim Tim!"

No answer. The penny whistle and the carols started up again, but as they did, a shadow appeared at the edge of the clearing. The whistle broke off mid-tweet, and then the singing faltered, and we children stopped playing. Fires crackled and wind jingled through the bells but no one said a word as the Timberman approached us, trudging through the snow with his axe in his hands.

He passed through the huddled groups of quiet, staring neighbors and stood beneath the tree. He smiled his bashful smile and then, looking up, he swung his axe over his shoulder, turned to us, and said, "Now."

He stepped forward and pulled the axe from off his shoulder. He lifted it high.

A voice called from the back of the crowd. "Not yet!"

The Timberman pulled back to swing, but paused when someone else cried, "Not yet!" He took another step toward the tree, and two more shouted "not yet", and then more joined in, and more, until we all stood around him, shouting, "Not yet! Not yet!"

He lowered his axe. Someone gave him a glass of cider and led him to one of the fires. Soon another group asked him to join them, and gave him more cider and this time a little brandy; and we all gathered around him, shaking his hand or clapping him on the back. Some of the girls gave him a peck on the cheek while we – the children – simply held onto his sleeves. The singing started again - cracked, badly done, sounding more like a flock of crows than people, and the woods rang with heartfelt song.

A great many Christmas Eve's have come and gone since then. The old spruce still stands on the mountain, though the Timberman is gone now, and my grandfather is gone, and most of those who sang that night are gone. No one puts lights on that tree any more, or hangs colored balls from its branches; but there are no more feuds. The fights, the arguments, the petty gossip – all the old battles faded as surely as the colored lights dimmed and went out. They have been replaced by new squabbles; mostly about the zoning laws and the size of the new school parking lot, but those old ones have been forgotten, with the old hatchets buried, and old water long since passed under the bridge.

They might have ended on their own. The distance between the argument over the '37 Chevy and the present day may have proved too great, and the threads of bitterness and resentment too weak. But still, whenever I think back through all the years, and all the Christmases, and bless each one I have spent in the company of those I have loved, I try to give special thought to the man who once loved a tree and made us all understand why.

Acknowledgements

In the 1930s, my grandparents hit upon the idea of making and selling wreaths to supplement their meager Depression-era wages. That was the start of what became the Christmas Barn, a gift shop set up in the vacant dairy stalls where they made things such as angels with Styrofoam ball heads, sequined eyes, and bodies made of large pine-cones – horrible looking things, though quite angelic to a child. For years one hovered at the top of our Christmas trees, with her cardboard wings and pipe-cleaner halo askew and, more often than not, one of her sequined eyes missing – which gave her a squint more befitting a pirate than an angel.

In no particular order I have these other memories… my mother turning all the lights out in the kitchen and sitting at the table for what seemed to be hours, drinking tea and gazing up at a small house on a hill, outlined in white light; lying in bed at my grandparents on Christmas eve, trying to stay awake, but feeling my eyelids grow heavier, heavier…a rumble approaches, a flashing light – is it Santa? No. The snow plow passes, its yellow light flashing and reflecting in the icicles and its great plow scudding over the road; coming downstairs – the tree – the gifts – Mickey the cat in the midst of them – and later, my father and grandfather packing up the back of a 1928 Model A truck with presents and kids, and taking us all to Aunt Pat's up on the ridge; the quiet, silent nights in the north woods…the hiss of falling snow…the scrape of a skate on ice, and sledding long after dark, up and down the hill, over and over…

Memories such as these form the heart of these stories. I never expected them to be gathered into a book. They began their lives as annual Christmas letters sent out to family and friends in lieu of cards, and I would like to thank those friends for all their support through all the years. I think of Bernadette Colas from Trinidad who, every single year, scolded me and said, "*Why* won't you put these in a book?" To Bern, I now say – "There. Happy now?" Other friends along the way were equally supportive and formed my "Christmas list": Tatsumi Fukunaga, Miss Dawn Hampton, Bobby Peaco, Diamond Lil, Aaron Lee Battle, Sean Haines, Alice Gallagher, Sza Cornelius and Tony, Hannah, Michael, Josh and Sam Starobin, Walt Jalbert and Jacqui Young, Ceil and Joe Carlucci, Eszti and K.C. Roehmer, Carol and John Burns, Warner and Dorie Peaco, Maggie Cullen and Karen Miller, Lily Cataldi, Lynne Randall, John Wilson, Richard Minor, Susan and Jerry Gabert, Walter Russell Mead, Tina Sloan; Alessandro, Kimm, Eleanor and Olivia Uzielli, Allegra

Ford, Massimo LaRocca, William Sievert, David Tucker, Rick Willett, Marcia "Cheech" Griffith-Pauyo; Michael, Melissa, Olivia and Jackson Walsh; Ted and Maggie Mills, Rose Roberts and the Dickensians, Bill McGinn and Christopher Baetz, Dale and Julia all the way over in Zambia, Challie Archila in Guatemala, Carlos Carmona from Columbia, Ronnie Ronquillo in the Philippines, Francesco Pireddu from Sardinia, Richard Dalton from "Dawchestah", and the one who above all others showed her appreciation over the years: Brenda West.

I thank my family too, always, for making every Christmas worthy of a story, starting with my parents, Joan and Edwin Thompson; my sister Karen and her husband Mitch, my brother Jim and his wife Stephanie, and the gang – Cameron, Lily, Sean, Emma and Mary-Kate. Special thanks go out to Aunt Pat and my partner in tree-decorating duty, Uncle Bob (both of whom also showed up on the dedication page, with good reason), Aunt Mary, Aunt Rita, and the Nova Scotia lasses, Marie and Corinne Cash, Marie and Eileen Donovan, Jane-Anne Sullivan, and all my many, many cousins too numerous to name, though Randy, Mary-Margaret, Kellie and Tom and their families must come in for special mention, as does my dear cousin and earliest friend Dianne Grant. Christmas present will always be linked to those of the past, and so I honor the memory of those with us in spirit only: my grandparents, John and Mary, and Mary and Joseph, Aunt Lib and the original Mrs. Cavanaugh, Dorothy Kirkland.

Now on to the book. I begin by thanking the two masterminds behind Osiail Publishing, author and marketing guru Phil McGrail and editor-extraordinaire, Josiah Eikelboom. They began Osiail as a home for Phil's first book, *Daughter of Statues*, and I am deeply appreciative of their enthusiasm and hard work on behalf of the Mink. I also thank Hillary Wentworth for poring over every comma, dash and misspelling; Ryan McCann, our graphic designer for putting up with our demands and throwing things together, despite it always being at the last minute; and Bob Tabian for his guidance and advice.

This book would be a far less lively affair without the artistry of my friend Jon Robyn. Jon and his faithful dog Max have tramped the woods where some of these stories are set, and his illustrations beautifully capture the spirit of our wintery tales. Thank you, Jon – thank you, thank you.

Finally, I come to two friends whose support through the years has made all the difference. The first, Bill Lloyd, has been a steadfast friend since my sailing days in the Virgin Islands, and I can never thank him enough for all he has done.

The second, Anne Ford, has been a loving friend and colleague, and gave me my first chance as co-author of her three books, *Laughing Allegra, On Their Own* and *A Special Mother*. My life would have been far less interesting and fun had I not met her by chance so long ago.

Lastly, I thank you, the one who now holds this book in your hands (or paws as the case may be). The memories I listed at the beginning of these acknowledgements are particular to me, and are no more valid than yours. I hope these stories brought back a sense of your own Christmas past – if not in the particulars, then in that hard to define feeling the Mink called "that warm shiver in your heart."

I wish you joy and good cheer for this and every Christmas.

John-Richard Thompson
St. Nicholas Day
December 6